The Fairy Child

J.D. MANDERS

authorHOUSE®

AuthorHouse™ LLC
1663 Liberty Drive
Bloomington, IN 47403
www.authorhouse.com
Phone: 1-800-839-8640

Cover Illustration by Susan Shorter
Interior Illustration by Lily Manders

Published by AuthorHouse 05/08/2014

ISBN: 978-1-4969-0562-8 (sc)
ISBN: 978-1-4969-0561-1 (hc)
ISBN: 978-1-4969-0560-4 (e)

Library of Congress Control Number: 2014907011

Contents

Preface

Evenings at our home were always a time of make-believe. Since my first daughter, Sarah, was three, we spent our nights immersed in childhood stories. Before she turned five, we had read *Peter Pan*, *Alice in Wonderland*, *The Wizard of Oz*, and *The Lion, the Witch, and the Wardrobe.* In between, we read the poetry of Robert Louis Stevenson or Christina Rossetti. When not reading, we would chase fireflies on the lawn, find shapes in the clouds in the evening sky, or watch the stars come out. Once Lily was born, my daughters and I continued the tradition of make-believe time. Not that this is in any way unusual. Many families, I am sure, have similar traditions.

In late 2003, I was called up to serve with the U.S. Army National Guard in Iraq. I was gone for more than a year, including mobilization, training, and demobilization. For the first time in my daughters' lives, we could not continue our tradition. With the unexpected and overwhelming demands of becoming a single parent and suffering from health problems, my wife understandably could not keep our tradition to the degree we had together. And no matter how I tried to convince them, no one in my unit seemed interested in make-believe time. It was a lonely period in my life, made even lonelier knowing that my children were pining away from lack of make-believe and time with their father. If only I could connect with them somehow and take part in their lives.

So it was that I conceived of writing a story for my children. Inspired by the many books we read in the past, I developed an outline in my mind. I made the stories about the adventures of two girls very similar to mine, also named

Sarah and Lily, whose father had also gone away to serve in the military. They were ordinary children who had an unusual adventure in which they learned to be brave in the face of disappointment and danger. This story seemed the perfect device to reach my children and instruct them in dealing with my absence. The story quickly came together. I finished the first chapter and sent it home for my wife to read to my children.

Naturally, as the story became more suspenseful, Sarah and Lily expressed concern about what was going to happen. Lily in particular wanted to make sure that the Lily in the story was safe after she disappeared at the end of the first section I sent home. They wanted another chapter, and I obliged them to ease their anxiety. Soon, they were out in the yard looking for fairies and wanted to know more about them. They wanted another chapter, and I sent another home. Of course, I could not write every day. I had missions to perform, and I traveled to other bases from time to time. However, the children were demanding. I quickly found myself spending every free moment I had writing or planning the story. I completed the entire manuscript in less than four months, feeding the chapters home every few days.

Soon, I heard, the story was being passed around to other children, to teachers, and to students. My children had told their friends about the story and played their fairy games with their playmates. On my return, my children's friends and teachers wanted a copy. These requests continued to increase. I finally decided that I should seek publication of the story, although I did not know how to do so. I received considerable help along the way. I wish to thank my daughters Sarah and Lily for their encouragement and for the original inspiration for writing the story. I deeply appreciate my wife Christy, who continually pushed and encouraged me in seeking publication. I also wish to thank

Edith Yeargin for editing support and numerous helpful comments. Most of all, I thank God for this opportunity and for such a wonderful family.

At the beginning, this story was written for two little girls—mine. Their personalities are only too clear to anyone who knew them at that time. Ultimately, however, they could have been about any two children. Many are placed in the terrible situation of being separated from a parent. They need the escape that only fiction can provide; they need to know that they can be brave. They are the true heroes of war for bearing this tremendous pain with such grace. It is in this spirit that I share what was a very personal story. I can only pray that, knowing its origins, the reader can overlook the flaws that resulted from its original purpose: its serial nature, its simplicity of structure and language, and its focus on one particular set of children.

J.D. Manders
November 2013

1

The Fairy Marketplace

How long fairies had been living in their back yard, Sarah and Lily did not know, but they knew they were there. Lily thought they had only been there a short time. After all, if there were people living in her yard, she would have seen them while she was out playing. She would have seen them under bushes or flying about in the moonlight. But Sarah thought they had been there a long time, and being older and well read, she was usually right about anything related to fairies or magic.

The girls had started noticing little signs of the fairies in the spring; signs that might be mistaken for natural occurrences if you did not know about the little people. Daddy had gone off to war in the fall, and as their mother was fighting off illness, the girls spent more and more time playing in the yard so as not to bother her. At first, the girls paid little attention to the fairy signs as they played because the signs were normal occurrences that anyone might see at any time—glowing snail trails or little animal footprints. By the fall, they had begun to put the signs together and finally started paying attention.

Some mornings, the yard was covered with a thick blanket of dew, and all children know that this is because the fairies were hard at work overnight. Mommy always tried to explain dew through science using words like condensation, but the children knew better. Dew meant that the fairies spilled their dust as they flew over the grass sprinkling moonlight around, and it turned to water in the morning sunshine. In the fall there was frost, when the snow fairies were about leaving wonderful streaks of white as they flew across the ground.

Then, the girls found fairy circles—little circles of mushrooms—after a spring rain. Lily had not seen these before, but Sarah had read about them.

"It's where the fairies were dancing around all night long," she explained. Sarah was always reading and knew a lot about the fairy folk. Nearly nine and with long brown hair and glasses, Sarah had been reading since she could hold a book in her hands. By this time, she had read all of the experts, from James M. Barrie to C.S. Lewis. "The fairies meet together and dance for hours playing their little instruments and flittering around. Where the fairies' feet touch the ground, mushrooms spring up. It's usually in a circle because they dance in a circle. You should never damage the circles. It's bad luck."

"Oh, I see," said Lily. As usual, she had found the mushrooms. She was the curious one that found out most things. Having just turned five, Lily had short blond hair to match her slight little body, and she was always climbing and reaching up under furniture to see what was there.

When Lily had shown the mushrooms to Mommy, Mommy said, "Don't go near them. They're a fungus." But Sarah's answer sounded better. It was the only logical explanation.

The next sign to appear was the lightning bugs. The girls often sat on the porch with Daddy before he went overseas. They would watch the bugs flying around in the twilight for countless minutes each evening. Sometimes they might even chase and catch the lightning bugs in a jar to make a firefly lantern. One night while sitting with Mommy, after Daddy had gone, the girls saw the bugs making patterns—faces and shapes. Sarah said that the only explanation was that the fairies were riding the bugs to line them up in a certain way. Naturally, Mommy did not see the faces in the glowing lights. They never could convince her.

If these were the only signs, the girls would have said that perhaps Mommy was right and that it could all be explained scientifically. Then one day, Lily found a little house at the foot of a tree behind some crab grass at the back of the yard. She went to get her sister.

"Sarah! Sarah!" Lily called. "I found a little house in the back yard. I think it's a fairy house."

"Where?"

"Under the little maple tree at the back of the yard, behind the daffodils. It's hard to see because it's behind the trunk."

The girls rushed to the back of the yard to take a look. They had a very large backyard for a house in the city. It was surrounded by a chain-link fence lined with crab grass and flowers. Behind the back fence ran an alley filled with bushes and trees that towered overhead. A gate opened along one side of the house from the front. There was a large tulip poplar tree in the center of the yard near the house that shaded the back patio and windows. At the back of the yard were a swing set and a miniature maple in the middle of a small flower garden.

The girls went straight to the back of the yard. Sure enough, there in a corner of the maple tree formed by two roots was a tiny roof thatched with pine needles using twigs as rafters. The walls were made of neatly cut and stacked pebbles glued with mud, while the door was made of pine bark cut into a square. There was even a small chimney that looked like the remains of an old, discarded wooden tobacco pipe. Steps made of sticks went up to the threshold, and going to the door was a worn path leading through the flowers near the tree.

"Wow!" Sarah exclaimed. "It has to be a fairy house. Can you see inside?" Sarah was pretty tall for being almost nine, so she was too big to see very well into the house because it was so near to the ground. Lily lay down on the grass and tried to peer into the front door. She was smaller and closer to the ground. It was dark inside, but Lily could see a rock table and a stool made from a slice of an old branch, like a small stump. She described what she saw.

"This must mean that the fairies have been in our yard for a while," Sarah said to her sister, who continued peering inside. "It must have taken time to build a house like that. There are probably many of them living in the area since they often live together. Is anyone at home?"

"I don't think so," Lily said. "And I don't think that anyone has lived here for some time."

"Why is that?"

"It's too dusty. In your books, the fairies always look so clean and bright. Have you ever heard of fairies being all dusty, I mean with real dust and not fairy dust?" Lily asked.

"That's true," Sarah replied, "but it may not be a proper fairy. It could be a gnome or an elf or maybe a brownie." Sarah was not exactly sure what a brownie was, but she had read of them in books and knew they were boys, and boys can be very messy.

"In any case," Sarah continued, "we know that some kind of fairy folk lived here at one time. The fairies probably know about our yard, that we don't have a dog, that Daddy is gone, and that it is a good place to meet."

Lily thought about the dog next door. Her family did not at that time have a pet. She did not like dogs herself, and she could see how dogs could scare away something as small as a fairy. The dogs probably chased the fairies as they chase squirrels and birds. But then, the fairies have magic and could turn the dogs into something else if they were too cruel.

"That is probably why we have seen so many fairy signs lately. Maybe one of them lived here at one point and knew the way. All we need to do is keep our eyes open, and I am sure we will see some fairies," Sarah explained.

As it turned out, Sarah was right, but not when they expected it. The girls started looking out for fairies, mostly flying around the flowers in the garden. They saw birds, bees, butterflies, and dragonflies, but never a pixie or sprite. As summer faded into fall, they watched for fairies in the sky among the falling leaves, for everyone knows that fairies love to ride the falling leaves down from the trees. Lily would jump and roll around in the piles of leaves just to see if the fairies were there. But they still had not seen any fairies until one warm autumn day.

Mommy had sent Sarah and Lily out to play so she could clean the house. It was an older, split-level house with a large set of stairs that made it difficult to clean. She had to lug the vacuum and other cleaning supplies up and down those stairs for hours, and it seemed every time she turned around the girls were underfoot. For this reason, Mommy always sent the girls outside to play when it was time to clean. At first, the girls went out to swing on their swing set since it was so warm and pleasant outside. Then they decided to kick a ball around. When Sarah kicked the ball under some bushes on one side of the yard, Lily nearly walked right into them. She leaned over to get the ball, and that's when she saw two small people about five or six inches tall walking under the crab grass along the fence.

Forgetting the ball, Lily started to walk behind the little people, but, not wanting to scare them, she moved quietly behind the corner of the house and watched them meander along. They were holding hands, smiling, and talking, although Lily could not hear their tiny voices. The little people walked along until they came to the hedgerow separating Sarah's and Lily's yard from their neighbor's, then the fairies disappeared under the branches. Afraid that she might lose track of them, Lily took a chance on being seen and peered under the bush.

To Lily's amazement, there were dozens of tiny colorful tents arranged in neat little rows. She saw a score of little people of all shapes and sizes. Some had wings, some didn't. A few rode on mice, birds, or other domesticated animals, but most were on foot. They were milling about talking and exchanging items. That's when Lily noticed that some had fruit or nuts; others had clothes made from rabbit or mouse fur. One was selling drinks by the barrel or glass. Another had tiny little jewelry all laid out on a table. One was telling fortunes. It was a fairy marketplace! All was carefully hidden by branches and leaves so that anyone could practically stand on top of the marketplace and not see it.

Now, by this time, Sarah began to wonder what had happened to Lily and started to look for her.

"Lily! Lily! Oh, there you are. What are you doing?" Sarah yelled.

Lily stepped away from the bushes until she was behind the house in the back yard. "Ssshh. You'll scare them away."

"Scare who away?"

"Why, the fairies, of course."

Sarah's mouth dropped opened, as did her eyes in an amazed stare. Even though Sarah believed in fairies, she did not really expect to find any. Fairies are very private people who are very good at hiding.

"Come and look," Lily said.

The girls crept back up to the bushes and got down on their hands and knees. Then Lily pulled back a low branch, and there the fairies were—the tents, the goods, and the fairy folk still bustling about buying and selling.

Later, the girls could not recall how long they stood there watching the fairies. It was entrancing. Once the girls had crept up to the bushes on their elbows and sat very still, they could hear some of the voices as they started to follow the scene more closely. There was an old man smoking a pipe and haggling over some jewels. In another corner, a young girl pixie was waiting tables at a tavern tent with red and white stripes. The bartender was in deep conversation about a hunting trip with a young man at the small wooden bar. In another corner, a young boy rode in on a mouse, dismounted, and tied up the steed to a branch. A woman collected several bags full of groceries from various tents, and then she mounted a robin and flew off to a tree in another yard. Each and every moment was fascinating.

At first, the girls worried that they might be seen and scare the little elves away. So they tried the best they could to hide behind branches and crab grass. The girls were as still and quiet as they could be. You would think that for little girls this would be practically impossible as wiggly as they often are. But the fairy marketplace was so entrancing the girls hardly said a word or moved an inch for several hours. Lily even forgot that she had to go to the bathroom.

Eventually, as the sun peaked in the sky, Mommy called for them to come in for lunch. They reluctantly obeyed, but decided that, now that they knew where the fairies were, they could find them again. Unfortunately, it turned rainy in the afternoon, as it often did in those late summer days when the heat of summer continued into autumn, and they did not get to go out and play again that day or the next.

Monday, after school, Lily went running to the side of the house, dropped her books, and got down on her hands and knees to look under the bush. There was nothing there but some dried leaves. She looked under the next bush, thinking she had looked under the wrong one, but there was still nothing. Lily looked up and down under all the bushes and in all the flowerbeds in the yard and still she found nothing. By this time, Sarah had come out. Lily was almost in tears after the frantic search.

"Sarah, the fairies are gone!"

"Let's try looking under the original bush," Sarah suggested.

They went back and scrutinized the ground. Sarah pointed out what looked like faint, square impressions in the grass—possibly where tiny tents had stood. Then Lily saw a teeny basket, empty of course, and an old stump like a stool. This was the place, all right, but all the fairies were gone.

"Well, perhaps they will be back," said Sarah, "but at least we know we were not crazy, and that the fairies were here. We just need to be patient."

The next day and the day after that, Lily looked again and again. She tired of looking and being disappointed. Lily had nearly decided to give up when Saturday rolled around again. After breakfast, the girls went out to play. Just out of curiosity, Lily looked again, and there were tiny people setting up tents and getting ready for another market day.

"Sarah, come and see!" Lily cried. "The fairies are back!"

"I told you they would come back," Sarah replied as the girls ran outside. After Sarah saw them setting up the tent, she added, "Oh, I see! Saturday must be market day. That is why the fairies are not here the rest of the week."

Sitting down again quietly, the girls watched the fairies begin their day putting up the tents and spreading out their goods on tables. At first, the fairies did not notice Sarah and Lily, perhaps because they were mostly behind the bush or perhaps because they were so quiet and still. Eventually, though, when the sun came up higher and began to cast shadows on the ground, one of the little men looked up and saw the girls. Several of the little people screamed and scurried about looking for cover. Most hid under the tents or ran into the bushes. Several others began to flee under the fence and across to the neighbor's yard.

I daresay that would have been the end of Sarah's and Lily's adventures—since no fairy was willing to come near them—but for a fortuitous event. About that time, the neighbor's dog Rusty ran out of the house near the bushes where the market was taking place. He was a large, red Labrador. Sensing the commotion, Rusty ran across the yard, barking and baying. Feeling trapped, the little sprites that were running across to the yard next door immediately ran back and began to look for a way out.

"The doggie," said Lily. "Sarah, make the doggie go away."

Sarah immediately got up and ran to intercept the dog. Knowing Rusty well, she grabbed the dog by the collar, pulled him back to the other side of the neighbor's house, and tied him to a leash wrapped around a post. Although the dog could run back and forth from the post to a tree, Rusty could not reach the fence or the market.

"Don't worry," Lily said quietly to the sprites, who peered out from under tents and baskets wondering what happened to the barking threat. "Sarah will tie Rusty up. I don't like dogs either. She won't let him hurt you."

Relieved, the little people began to come back out into the open. After making sure the coast was clear, they started back to work setting up the tents and laying out their things. A few still looked up cautiously at the giant who was watching their proceedings. One old gnome went up to Lily. He was about five inches tall with a long white beard. He was evidently a fairy of some importance. He waved his hand for Lily to come nearer. She bent her head down to listen.

"My dear little girl, thank you for saving us from that vicious cur."

Lily looked questioningly at him.

"The dog. Thank you for getting rid of the dog. We are sorry that we were so scared of you. We always have to be careful around big people. You never know what they are going to do. They are so clumsy and stupid and mean—not you personally, that is. So many are concerned only with money or fame. But you have done us a great service without expecting anything in return. For being so helpful, I name you and your sister elf-friend. You are welcome to join us. I will explain to the others."

The gnome went off and began to talk to the others, and the other fairies all nodded their heads in approval. So it was that when Sarah got back, Lily was helping set up tents and moving furniture around like they were in her dollhouse, talking lively to the little people about her dolls and the fairy market. Sarah sat down, too, and Lily explained the whole situation.

After the girls helped set up, they talked to several of the patrons. Most of the fairies were very curious about the lives of big people, and wanted to know what they did, how old they were, where and how they lived, what kind of magic they worked, and so forth. In return, the girls learned quite a bit about the fairy folk, starting with the difference between elves and gnomes, sprites and pixies, brownies, and leprechauns. They learned that the market had been meeting in their yard for months, and that, in fact, fairies lived all over that part of the city. Sarah found this particularly amazing. It was one thing for fairies to live in the woods away from everyone and be able to remain hidden, but to live right there among big people under the very eaves of their houses and never be seen was nothing short of remarkable. It was only through magic that the fairies could remain hidden under these circumstances. Sarah wondered whether she and Lily had some special resistance to their magic (as some pure-hearted children do), whether they were extremely lucky to have come across them, or whether perhaps there was more than an element of chance involved.

The girls continued talking to the fairies throughout the day. They mostly talked to the little people, but occasionally they would pick up and look at items for sale when asked. Lily stroked a fur coat to ensure it was genuine, and Sarah held up a beautiful necklace—the size of a ring to her—to examine its beauty. After lunch they came out again to play in the yard and spent the whole time doing nothing but playing with the fairies. Occasionally, the fairies would offer the girls food, but for some reason, Sarah would always refuse and insist that Lily do the same. Lily thought perhaps that it was because they had nothing to offer in return and did not want to seem rude.

Soon, the sun began to dip below the trees, and the shadows grew long. Some of the fairies began to pack their things to return to fairyland. Suddenly, Mommy called for Sarah. She ran quickly inside to find out what her mother wanted.

"Are you sure you would not like some fruit?" one little fairy asked Lily, seeing that she was hungry and licking her lips.

"Maybe just one," Lily said. She reached down to the young woman's bin and picked a berry. She bit into it, and it was the juiciest little blueberry she had ever put into her mouth. She picked another from the stack and another.

"Where is Lily?" Mommy asked Sarah when she ran inside.

"She is still outside playing," Sarah said.

"Well, it is almost dinnertime. Please go get her."

Sarah ran out of the house and back to where she and Lily had been sitting. Lily had disappeared, and so had the market. Sarah checked under the bush where the market had been. There was not a basket or sign left. With dark falling, the fairies had probably packed up for the night. But where was Lily?

"Lily!" Sarah called out over and over again, looking all around the house. She looked under every tree and bush. Thinking that maybe Lily had followed the fairies home, it dawned on Sarah. The fairies had kidnapped Lily!

2

The Kingdom of Fairie

Lily was gone with the fairies, leaving Sarah behind to explain everything to Mommy. Sarah began to think. Mommy would not believe the story about the fairies unless there was some scientific evidence left behind, but there wasn't any. She had already looked. Anyway, it would be better to get Lily back before Mommy noticed she was gone. As small as the fairies were, they could not have gone far in such a short time. They must be close by, perhaps in a neighboring yard. She spent several minutes looking under all the bushes and in the flower gardens in the yards nearby for Lily. When Mommy called, Sarah had to go back inside.

"Where is Lily?" Mommy asked.

"She's out playing with the fairies and did not want to eat," Sarah said, though she knew that this was not completely true.

"Fairies, huh? That sounds like a fun game. Well, she must eat something. Take this bag of carrots and crackers out to her."

Sarah diligently obeyed, even though she knew she would not find Lily. She knew she ought to tell her mother everything, but felt like she would be blamed, and perhaps rightfully. After all, Sarah was the one who had left Lily in the yard by herself with the fairies. Besides, she still thought she could get Lily back in time. Sarah sat down on the edge of the porch and tried to think of how to get out of this mess.

Where could Lily have gone? Sarah tried to think about the day and all they had discussed. Suddenly, she remembered Lily asking for food. She had told Lily not to eat anything, but maybe Lily did it anyway. Daddy had once read them a story about two little girls who went to a goblin marketplace and ate some of their food only to become entranced. The goblins were going to take them away forever. Goblins were like evil fairies—they were small and very wicked, but their magic was similar. Obviously, Lily had eaten some of the fairy food, and they took her away. Since Sarah could not find the fairies and Lily was not one to wander off on her own, it was the only explanation that made sense. Sarah remembered the fairies asking them a lot of questions. Did they live alone? Had they ever been away from home? Were they hungry? They kept asking again and again. The more Sarah thought about it, the more the whole episode with the fairy marketplace and the dog seemed like a planned abduction. She just did not know the reason why.

But how could Sarah get Lily back? She did not know where the fairies had gone or what direction. She looked at the ground, hoping there would be fairy dust or some kind of glowing trail in the twilight that would lead her, but there was nothing. The fairies could have used magic to hide their tracks, in which case Sarah would find nothing. She examined all the trees for fairy houses, but did not see anything suspicious, although the fairies could have easily hid their homes with magic. Sarah's only clue was the marketplace itself, which would not be back for another week. Sarah could not stall Mother for a whole week, she just couldn't! But was she sure they only came on Saturday? Last week, it rained on Sunday. Maybe the marketplace was open all weekend. It was her only hope.

A plan began to formulate in Sarah's mind. She would stall Mother until morning and then come out early to look for Lily. She could then track Lily down or force the fairies to tell her where Lily was. If Sarah was wrong, and the market was not open on Sunday, she would break down and tell her mother.

Sarah went back inside and told her mother that she would put Lily to sleep. Now that Sarah was older, Mommy often asked her to do this when feeling ill, so it was no surprise that Sarah would volunteer. Sarah put a teddy bear under the sheets to make it look like Lily was there and turned out the light. Then, she went to her own room and began to prepare. If the fairies took Lily far away, Sarah would need to be ready for a journey. She got her little backpack that she took camping and started getting some useful things together. Sarah took Lily's bag of food and went to the kitchen and prepared a bag for herself. She packed some extra clothes for herself and then for Lily. What else do you need when you travel? Rope is always useful, so Sarah went to the garage and found a coil of rope, which she promptly packed. What if it got dark? She had better pack a flashlight, she thought, so Sarah went to the bathroom and pulled one from under the sink that Daddy had stored in case the lights went out.

Everything was ready. Now, Sarah just needed to sleep. She prayed especially hard that night that God would keep Lily safe, and that she would be able to find her. Then Sarah went to sleep and slept as only children can in the face of such worry.

As soon as the sun was up, she dressed, grabbed her pack, and went out to play in the backyard.

"Please be there, please be there, God, let her be there," she prayed over and over again as she ran outside.

Sarah went straight to the bushes and sighed a sigh of relief. There were the fairies again, putting up the tents and getting ready for another market day. Sarah greeted the fairies, who by now were used to her being there and did not scare at all.

"Have you seen my sister?" Sarah asked.

"We saw her yesterday here at the market," one girl pixie answered.

"Did you see where she went? She did not come home last night, and Mommy will be oh so very worried."

The woman started to say something, but the old gnome stepped between them and said, "No, we have not seen her since yesterday. Maybe some human took her."

Sarah had not thought of this, but it could be true. There were a lot of mean people that might take a little girl, especially when she was in her yard by herself. However, everything else pointed to the fairies. Lily was with them. The fairies had offered her their magical food. The fairies had to take her, but why would they lie about it? Why would they need her at all? Maybe the fairies needed big people to help with some task back at their kingdom. If so, Sarah had to convince them that Lily was not the right one. So, she came up with another plan.

"Lily is so little," Sarah began. "She can hardly take care of herself. She is so young. That is why I am so worried about her. She would be useless in the face of danger. I mean, she's scared of dogs, for Pete's sake."

The little gnome looked thoughtful. "Yes, but Lily's so big," he said. "And she said yesterday that she had learned to dress herself. I am sure that she will be okay."

"I am usually there to watch over her. We do everything together. If Lily had her sister there, she would be very brave, but by herself, she would be very frightened. And you would think that whoever took her would know that two little girls are always better than one."

The little gnome stroked his beard and puffed on his pipe as though he were very deep in thought.

"My, but where are my manners," he said slyly. "You have probably not eaten breakfast. What you would be wanting is some food. How about some nice fruit?"

He motioned to the girl pixie, and she came forward with a small plate of berries.

"I would not mind if I do," Sarah said. She reached out and grabbed a handful. She smiled politely, then turned her head and acted like she was taking a bite. Sarah broke the berry and rubbed the juice on her chin, but was careful not to actually eat any. Then she put the remainder of her handful of berries into her pocket.

Sarah continued to talk and act as though she were eating their food and drinking their drink, all the while never actually eating or drinking anything. That way, she thought, she would not fall under their spell and could get away if she needed. But Sarah would have to act as though she were under a spell.

It was a pleasant day, and the conversation was very interesting. Sarah learned more than she had the previous day. She learned that these particular fairies all were part of the same kingdom under their magnificent queen, Selena. But because she was so worried about Lily, Sarah did not really enjoy her time with them as she had the previous day. As the day wore on, Sarah became more and more anxious for the day to end, so she could find Lily. In fact, she was afraid that she would run out of time. Any moment, her mother would come out looking for her and Lily, and she would be shocked to find just Sarah in the yard.

It started to get darker as the sky threatened rain once more. Wind began to blow, and the fairies began to quickly pack up their things. Sarah could hear her mother calling from inside for them to come in before the rain.

Just then, the old gnome said, "Sarah, it is time to go. You will go with us. When you get to our kingdom, you can have all the food and drink you want. We must go quickly before the grown-up comes outside."

Overjoyed that her plan had worked so well, Sarah struggled to look troubled as she thought someone being kidnapped by fairies might look. Inside, she was happy that she would soon find Lily. At the same time, she was nervous that her mother might find out. Sarah tried to act upset, looked back at her house once or twice, but obeyed.

The sprites finished packing the tents and loaded them onto the backs of mice and rabbits. Several fairies flew off in different directions, while those without wings started on a caravan across the neighbor's yard, straight for the tree line in the alley behind the lot. Sarah walked slowly along with them. The wind began to blow, and she could see the dark clouds rolling in, covering the sky. Sarah saw lightning and began to be afraid, but still the fairies pressed forward, moving toward a giant stump at the back of the lot.

As the fairies reached the tree line, Sarah could hear her mother come out the back door, calling for them. She was suddenly tempted to call out to her mother. She could not ignore her mother. Mommy would know exactly what to do. Mommy was so strict that the fairies would obey her and bring Lily back. Mommy could save them all, even now.

Sarah turned her head, but she held her tongue because she noticed that everything was getting bigger. The trees nearby looked enormous, like the California Redwood trees she had heard about from her uncle. The grass, which had moments ago looked small and neatly trimmed now looked like long savanna grass in Africa, waist-high. The house looked like a mansion, then a skyscraper. Her mother grew farther and farther removed, first like a giant touching the sky, then like some billboard miles away. Sarah wondered how the fairies were making the world grow while they stayed the same. Then she realized, everything was not getting bigger; Sarah was shrinking. It was the fairies' magic at work that made everything appear this way.

Sarah turned her head back and saw that she was now the same size as the fairies. She tried calling to her mother, but her mother did not hear. Sarah's voice was now a tiny peep, sounding like a cricket's chirp or a bird's shrill call. She started to run back toward her mother and the house, but one of the fairies caught her and said something to her. Sarah could not hear over the wind and the distant thunder. The gnome herded her onto a cart being pulled by a white rabbit and closed the gate behind her. The rails of the cart were as tall as her shoulders. Sarah jumped up and leaned over the rails, but she could not escape.

Sarah turned to see where the fairies were taking her. They were moving toward the old stump at the back of the yard. Daddy had cut the tree down many years ago, but it stood well over a foot tall. All of the other fairies were moving toward it. She could see lights twinkling around the outside of the stump, as though there were tiny windows all over it. Even for the fairies, it seemed somewhat small.

Ahead was a dark hole. It was not a real hole, but simply a black patch in front of them obscuring all else. As there was no depth to it, it had to be magical. Sarah and the fairies moved into the blackness, and soon lights began to swirl around them, forming a sort of tunnel. The sky and grass behind them faded to nothingness. After a while, the lights ahead of them began to stay in one place. Initially, the lights were as distant as stars, but they moved steadily closer until Sarah saw that they were real lights—candles, lanterns, torches, and fires. She could see people moving around them. Soon, she saw that the lights were all in a wondrous banqueting hall, as big as the largest cave she had ever seen. As she moved closer to it, Sarah got a better look.

The hall was enormous, with a huge wooden ceiling larger than any church sanctuary. It was made of the most exquisitely carved wood. Sarah could see faces and figures with swirling designs carved into the walls. There appeared to be at least five levels to the hall, each with row after row of arches and hallways radiating back to other rooms and halls. Between each arch was a torch. From the ceiling hung several wooden chandeliers, making the hall bright and cheery. The roof was very distant, but appeared to be a large, golden dome. Sarah could only guess that this was the palace of the Kingdom of Fairie, of which the old gnome had spoken.

There was a huge crowd of fairies in the hall—elves, pixies, gnomes, sprites, and even a leprechaun or two. Some were seated eating at candlelit tables. Some were gathered around large circular fires warming their hands. Others appeared to be dancing to marvelous music of violins and flutes coming from some unseen source over her head. Sarah looked up and saw balcony after balcony packed with people watching and waving, and flying overhead was a host of fairies dancing in the air, flying back and forth to the music. It was like a ball, but stretched across the air on many levels. At the back of the hall, there was a great mass of people waiting for a seat. It was a feast to end all feasts.

The fairies entered the hall and quickly dismounted the mice and rabbits, as fairy stable hands came and took the animals away to rest. Sarah looked behind where the darkness was but saw only the wooden wall of the hall behind her. The magic gateway had closed. She could not go back that way.

The old gnome began to lead the party toward the front of the room. The group pushed through fairies dancing or standing around talking. Along the way, Sarah saw table after table full of food. At the very front of the hall on a raised stage was a long banqueting table lit by beautiful golden candelabras with places all set out with the finest china and silverware. At the head table, richly dressed guests were sitting and eating politely. But one guest seemed to be dressed more sumptuously than the others, and everyone was treating her with the greatest respect. She wore a flowing white gown with patterns of roses sewn into it. She had long, blond hair with a tiara of gold and diamonds on her head. Sarah's eyes turned toward her, expecting a queen or fairy. Lily looked up at her.

3

The Fairy Queen

"What are you doing here?" Sarah asked Lily.

"Eating," Lily said.

"No, I mean, how did you get here?" Sarah replied.

"They said if I went with them, they would give me more food, so I went. They gave me my own room, these beautiful clothes and jewelry, and they call me Princess Lily."

"Did they hurt you or try to make you do anything?" Sarah asked.

"No. I am okay. It's really great here. They tell the most wonderful stories, and the food is really good. It must always be somebody's birthday because they have parties every night."

"What do you mean, 'every night'? It's just been one night since you left."

"Maybe at home, but here it has been nearly a week. Anyway, my room is really big, and I get to sleep in a bed with a canopy. It's like going camping every night. They even said I could go hunting with them. I get to ride a horsy and go out into the woods. It will be just like camping with Mommy and Daddy."

"Speaking of Mommy, you had us worried to death."

"I'm sorry. I really did not think of that. I just wanted more of the food, and, well, to be with the fairies. I am glad you are here, now. Mommy would never have believed me that all of this happened," Lily said as she stood up and embraced Sarah.

"Well, I suppose now that I am here, I should join the party."

"Yes, they said only moments ago that they were expecting you. I asked that they let us share a room. Let me show you where it is. They have put out your clothes for the party tonight."

Lily excused herself from the table like a good little girl and showed Sarah across the great hall, through one of the archways, up some winding stairs, along a little hallway decorated with pictures and tapestries, and through a little wooden door. The room was even lovelier than Lily described. It was spacious and had lots of antique furniture. There were now two beds with canopies, two nightstands, several chairs, a writing desk in one corner, a bookshelf with some old books, two wardrobes, a large oval mirror on a stand, a small table with a chess board on it, and four brass candelabras with candles, one on each side of each bed. There was a window, but the shutters were closed. Sarah tried them, but they were locked from the outside. In any case, their room was several stories above the ground. It was no use trying to escape that way.

Lily opened one of the wardrobes and said, "Here's a dress for you. They really have pretty clothing here. I think someone told me that they hand-sew all of them. There's some jewelry, too, anything you might want. It's like playing dress-up, only with real outfits."

Sarah put on the dress and matching shoes and picked another tiara with matching earrings (clip on) and pendant necklace. She also put on a gold bracelet. She stood in front of the mirror and looked at herself. Sarah looked like a grown-up princess with all that finery. But she would only just fit in with the other guests, who were all dressed in finery.

While Sarah waited on Lily to freshen up, she looked about the room. The books looked rather old and uninteresting until she opened one up, a history of Ireland. Inside was a very realistic picture of some battle. As she looked at it, she saw movement. The people in the picture were moving about, like it was a television. Sarah watched for a few moments as two armies charged each other, amazed at this bit of magic. She closed the book. Curious, she opened it again, and the battle was back at the beginning. Sarah flipped through the book and found several other pictures, all of which moved in the same way. After she put down the book, she looked at the chessboard. It looked ordinary enough. Sarah tried to remember the rules of chess that Daddy tried to teach her, but the pieces would not move. It was as if they were glued to the board. Suddenly, Lily reappeared.

"How do you make the pieces move?" Sarah asked.

"Oh, one of the ladies in waiting showed me. 'Knight to king's bishop three,'" Lily commanded. The piece slowly moved on its own until it was in the position named. "I don't know what that means, but that is what the lady said to make it move."

"It's getting pretty dark in here. I suppose we should get someone to light the candles," Sarah wondered out loud.

"No need," Lily said. Then moving in front of one of the candelabras, she commanded, "Candles light." Flames magically appeared. "Everything is magic here. I guess it's because of the fairies. Now, let's get back to the party. The queen is supposed to be here tonight."

"Queen, huh? That's exactly who we need to talk to."

They returned to the banquet hall, and a place at the head table had been cleared for Sarah next to Lily. Sarah did not eat anything for fear of coming under the fairies' spell, which would make her never want to leave, although she did take a chance and drink some plain water. That would probably be safe enough. Instead of eating the sumptuous food, Sarah munched on some of the carrots and fruit that she had brought with her. She soon became absorbed with socializing and forgot all about being hungry. Mostly, however, Sarah listened to the stories of all the guests and looked in wonder about that marvelous place.

At one point, one of the elves stood up and began to tell a story about a beautiful unicorn. A young maiden fell in love with the unicorn, spending hours playing with it. But the maiden was accused of being a witch because the animal came when called as if enchanted. At the last moment, the unicorn took her place and was put to death before her eyes, only to return from death and meet her in the orchard to ride off together. Unicorns, it seems, were immortal. The father of the maiden tried to hunt down and kill the unicorn, but the maiden and the unicorn escaped into a neighboring kingdom, where they dwelt together until the end of her days. This story met with nods of approval from everyone as though it were a court favorite.

Following this tale, a leprechaun told a story of a man trying to steal his gold. The leprechaun tricked the man into putting on magic shoes that made him dance until near death, when he gave up his hunt for the gold. The three or four leprechauns in the room applauded loudly, but most of the other fairies only clapped politely at its conclusion.

"The leprechauns and dwarves are always telling stories about gold, which they care a lot about but doesn't interest most of the other fairies," Lily whispered to Sarah.

Then, one of the fairies began to tell a story in honor of their guests. Two girls from the Old Country (that was what they called England) once found fairies in their yard and began to talk about it so much that grown-ups began to come from all over the country to try to prove that the fairies did exist by capturing some. One man, a famous magician named Houdini, headed the effort by bringing ladies' clubs, reporters, and government officials. The girls even produced photographs of the fairies. The people ransacked the yard, destroyed the flower garden, and tracked mud all over the house. Later, the girls told everyone that they had made the fairies in the photos using paper dolls pinned to trees and flowers. The crowds then went away. Only then did the girls return to the fairies, which were real after all. The point was obvious—most grown-ups can't see fairies and make too much of a fuss about them, so the girls should be careful which grown-ups they tell.

Next came the dancing. A band with a fiddler, a flutist, a lute player, an upright bass, and a percussionist with tambourines played from one of the balconies. The music was mostly old Celtic music from the Old Country, which was lively and joyful. Most of the people danced little Irish jigs, which Sarah always wanted to learn. You had to keep your hands at your side while kicking up your feet above your knees. Sarah had seen them dance like that on television. But after the leprechaun's story, she was afraid of being enchanted and dancing all night long, so she just watched enthusiastically.

All during the time she was enjoying the party, Sarah looked about the room for a way outside to her yard. Pretending that she was watching the dancing, she wandered about the hall looking for an exit. Lily might be enchanted, but Sarah was not and could grab Lily and run if the opportunity presented itself. First, Sarah casually moved to the side of the room where she came in to examine the wall, but she found no trace of a door. Not even a crack. The fairies had used magic to open an entrance that was not really there. On another side of the room, Sarah saw a large pair of double doors, which must have been the main entrance. She moved in front of the doors, placing her hands behind her back. Then she tried the door handle quietly so as not to arouse suspicion, but the doors appeared to be locked, as she could not budge them. In short, there appeared to be no way out. Sarah and Lily were locked inside the palace.

Once or twice, Sarah excused herself to go to her room as a ruse to find some way out of the palace, but the halls were winding and confusing, and she found herself getting lost. Finally, Sarah turned down a hall that she thought went deeper into the palace, but she ended back in the banquet hall.

This is not right, Sarah thought, so she went back to her last turn and went the opposite direction, but still ended up back in the main hall. She tried several other archways and halls, all with the same effect. No matter which way Sarah turned, she always ended up in the main hall. It must be enchanted, she thought. After several tries, she never found an exit aside from the main doors in the hall. Finally, Sarah gave up and returned to her seat.

"How do you get back to our room if you always return to this hall?" Sarah asked Lily.

"Oh, the fairies say you always get to the place you want the best by going in the opposite direction. It took me a while to learn how to do it, but you have to try to return to the hall to make it to your room."

"How confusing," Sarah said. "It must take an awful lot of concentration to do anything here. Getting up at night to find the bathroom must be a terrible ordeal."

Not long after Sarah returned to the table, two trumpeters appeared near one of the doors to announce the arrival of Queen Selena. The people stood and became very quiet. The double doors opened, and a brilliant light came from outside glowing brightly into the room. A beautiful fairy appeared in the door dressed in white and wearing a crown. In her hand was a wand. Her wings folded against her back as she entered the room. Everyone bowed or curtsied before her. As she proceeded into the hall, the people politely moved out of her way, forming a path to the head table. The queen walked gracefully into the room.

As the queen approached the head table, Sarah and Lily stood and curtsied as Mommy had taught them. The old gnome who had brought Sarah approached respectfully.

"Your majesty, may I introduce the human children, who are powerful princesses among their people, and who have been named elf-friends because of services performed. This is Princess Sarah the Dog Killer and Princess Lily the Fairy Guard. Sarah and Lily, may I present Selena, Queen of Fairie, Jewel of the Pixies, Sovereign of Sprites, Arch Duchess of Fairy Land."

Sarah and Lily curtsied again, bowing their heads.

"I thought there was only one human child, Gnicholas," Selena said to the gnome.

"We originally brought only one child, Lily, but because of her youth, we decided to bring her sister to comfort and help her," he replied.

"I did not approve this. Still, I believe you have decided correctly. Two little girls are always better than one, and you have evidently picked the bravest and strongest human children within the bounds of our kingdom."

"Excuse me, your majesty," said Sarah. "But we are not that brave. And we are not really princesses, except maybe to Daddy. We are just ordinary little girls from an ordinary family. We have never done anything important or courageous."

"But did you not vanquish the dog and save our people?" Selena asked.

"It was just Rusty, and all I did was tie him up. It was really not that brave."

"Your modesty befits those born of high rank," said Selena.

"It is not just that. You see, we were taken from our mother and home and miss them terribly. Aren't there other, braver children you would want?"

Selena looked at the old gnome, who said, "They are the only children within the bounds of our kingdom that we have found inside ten years who actually believe in fairies. Children are made to grow up too quickly nowadays, and since grown-ups don't believe in us, children suffering from this malady are of no use to us. Of the other children I observed, they either did not believe in us, or were sickly, or were guarded too carefully for us to approach. No, your majesty, these were the only children available. Aside from this fact, there is also the matter of the signs we saw on Sarah and Lily that none of the other children possessed."

"And what signs are these?" Selena asked.

"Signs that they are themselves related to fairy folk, your majesty. There is the matter of Lily's blond hair and brown eyes, a unique combination found primarily among fairies. And then there are Sarah's ears, not quite pointed, but obviously of elvish air. We were sure based on these signs that the children were the ones we need and that they would help."

"These are very strong reasons," said Selena.

"But you enchanted Lily and stole her," Sarah said, becoming more bold as she grew angry at being discussed casually as though she were not there. "You certainly have not treated us like people whose help you need, but like prisoners."

"For that, we are sorry," said Selena. "I did not know all of the details of your being brought here. It is true that sometimes we must rely on nontraditional means of persuasion, but we always give you a choice. However, you can be sure that our intentions are good, and that we will not harm you nor keep you from your family longer than is necessary to fulfill your mission."

"That is another question we have," said Sarah. "I guessed that you took us for a reason, but no one has explained the reason to us or given us a chance to decide whether to help or not."

"There was a reason, but we could not have explained it since we did not know you and did not know whether you would or could help us or whether we could even talk to you rationally. It was for the reason of discussing the mission that we brought you here, that and to prepare you. You must understand that ordinarily, we avoid all contact with the human world. It always contains a risk of being discovered, cheated, tricked, or badly misused. However, this particular task requires the aid of humans because of enchantments that prevent fairy folk from completing it. But if we must get children, we must look for those who believe, those who are honest and would not betray our trust, and those who are good-hearted enough to help. As Gnicholas explained, this was why he chose you."

"We are certainly flattered," Sarah said, "but our mother will miss us too much to be gone even overnight from our home. We must refuse simply because of that."

"On that account, you need not worry. We have placed a spell that makes time move very slowly for your mother while your time here moves at normal speed. Even if you were gone several days, your mother would not miss you more than a few minutes."

"That would explain the discrepancy of time that Lily described," Sarah said to herself. "To those in the real world, days seem like hours, and hours like minutes."

Lily, who had been listening to their talk for some time, finally pulled at Sarah's dress and said, "Sarah, I like it here. I don't want to go."

Selena smiled and looked to see Sarah's response.

"Of course she wants to stay," Sarah said, "She is under your spell. But I am not because I never ate your food."

The old gnome looked surprised, but the queen seemed to know it all along.

"That is true, and you are free to leave at any time. But please stay and listen to our story. There is no harm in that. If you decide after that point to leave, we will release Lily from the spell of the food and allow her to go with you. It will do you no harm to stay until you have heard us out. Now, please, eat and drink so you will be refreshed and may pay attention. You need not fear. The food here is not enchanted."

"Very well," said Sarah. "We do thank you for the good time and the clothes and all. At the very least, we owe you the time you ask."

So, Sarah sat down and finally ate. Fairies flew out and helped clear the hall and brought fresh table settings in for the queen and her personal guests. Lily was overjoyed. She sat at the table and finished her dessert, being careful to use her napkin to wipe her face like polite girls should. After Sarah and Selena had finished, the servants brought in the fine china and poured them each a cup of tea. Imagine, thought Lily, a tea party with real fairies! It was much better than a tea party with dolls or stuffed animals.

As they sipped the tea listening politely, Selena began to tell her tale.

4

The Fairy Queen's Tale

"I came into my kingdom early, and there have always been challenges to my rule," began Queen Selena as she told her tale. "You see, many years ago, each of the fairy folk had their own kingdoms and rulers."

"Are there more than one fairy folk?" asked Lily.

"I forgot for a moment that you are humans and have little knowledge of our world. Yes, there are elves, pixies, gnomes, brownies, leprechauns, and dwarves. It is said that fairies came from the angels at the beginning of time and degenerated from there, but that is a long story. In any case, each of the fairy peoples had their own rulers, as I said. The elves ruled the elves. The dwarves ruled the dwarves. That was how it was for many centuries. As people began to look for the fairies to subject them to science, and creatures of evil began to attack them with increasing frequency because gentility has gone out of the world, the individual tribes were easy prey. So it was that all the fairy folk came together at what was called the Grand Fairy Council only a little more than a hundred years ago according to your reckoning, although it was much longer in our world. At that time, the representatives from all the fairy peoples decided that a single ruler would help unite the fairy folk against our common enemies and help coordinate and communicate between the different fairy peoples.

"Many of the fairy folk worried about losing their independence, so it was decided that the ruler would only decide on matters concerning all of them—such as defense, territorial disputes, or trade. All other decisions would be left to the individual kings—the leprechaun king, the gnome chieftain, the elf lords, the dwarf king, and so forth. Because of people's fears, it was important to choose an overlord that would not be a tyrant and try to enslave the people or usurp their rights. Several of the rulers of the individual tribes were immediately discounted or else withdrew themselves from consideration. The dwarf king and leprechaun king, for instance, were too concerned with their own affairs, mining tunnels or amassing wealth, while the woodland elves did not want the responsibility because they were so flippant and carefree.

"After considering several rulers, it finally came down to two. The first was Fiara, an elf who had proclaimed herself the queen of the brownies, and so claimed the allegiance of two of the peoples. Of course, the elves did not recognize Fiara as their queen, but she had a large following among them, and they supported her for overlord because she had second sight. They argued that this gift would be useful in protecting the kingdom because Fiara could see enemies coming before they arrived. Also, her magic was very strong. The brownies followed Fiara because she gave them more power than they would have had on their own, for their magic more concerns hiding and playing tricks than making war. The brownies were not really leaders, and Fiara was able to easily sway them.

"Then, there was my father, the oldest of fairies. He was nearly five hundred years old and was well known to fairies on both sides of the ocean, having been one of the first fairies to come from the Old Country."

"Wow!" interjected Sarah. "Five hundred years old. Our country has not even been around that long."

"Yes," the Fairy Queen continued. "As you know, most fairy peoples live for hundreds of years unless they die in war or in accidents. My father actually came over with one of the first pilgrims to this country and made peace with the sprites that already lived in this land."

Sarah guessed that she meant the nature spirits that the Indians always believed in and sometimes wrongfully worshipped. Selena continued:

"Those who supported my father argued that fairies were fast and could travel easily from people to people, making them more dispensable than the other peoples for this kind of job. His magic was also strong, though in a different way—he had powers to hide and to disappear, by which he might keep the fairies hidden. Those who favored open warfare against the Big People wanted Fiara, and those who favored hiding our kingdoms favored my father. But mostly, the council decided, the position was a political one. All of the fairies needed someone who could pull the people together, someone who could be trusted, someone respected enough the others would listen. My father was old, wise, and widely respected, which gave him the edge, while Fiara was young and ambitious. Ultimately, there was only one choice."

"Your father," Sarah said.

"Exactly—my father became the Archduke of Fairy Land, which is what they called the collected fairy kingdoms. He was a good ruler, and the first years of the new kingdom went well, but soon two events created a breach. The first was that Fiara left the kingdom in protest of not being selected as duchess. I was there when she announced she was removing herself from the kingdom. I remember it like it was yesterday. Fiara came before the council and said, 'You have chosen foolishly. Very well, I will leave the kingdom, and lift my protection from it. You will see how long you can survive without my help, and then perhaps you will reconsider. I foresee that one day you will ask me again to be queen. Only then shall I return.' Then, she stormed out. Since that time, we have understood that what she meant was that she would cause as many problems as she could until we relented.

"Although Fiara still maintains contact with several fairy peoples, mostly the brownies and dark elves, she went to live among men. Humans call her a witch because of her magical powers. Fiara used her magic to change her appearance, and some have said that she even has goblins working for her now, which shows the depths to which she has fallen, for they are an evil race. Fiara started harassing the fairy folk, insisting that she is the rightful queen. There have been several fairies, elves, and gnomes that have disappeared when traveling near her domain, presumably imprisoned, killed, or enchanted.

"The other event that has crippled the new arrangement was the death of my father. Not many years after his selection, my father was attacked by wolves in the woods and was unable to fly away. Since no one was around to witness it, a lot of questions have continued to surround his death, so that many people believe he was murdered. Some have wondered how wolves could approach him so stealthily, or else they wonder how my father was trapped on the ground so that he could not fly away. Most now believe that some kind of magic was involved, which implicates Fiara. Unfortunately, nothing was ever proved."

"How terrible!" Sarah said. Lily looked in wonder. "A wolf is like a big dog," Sarah explained, and Lily gasped.

"So it was that I became queen at a young age. Some immediately opposed my elevation, but they were mostly supporters of Fiara, and these soon left the assembly. Most, however, continued to support me because of sympathy for my father. It has been difficult, to say the least. Always there has been strife, attacks on the fairy folk, and threats from Fiara. But the big obstacle is that a male heir was wanted, so the throne would stay within our family and provide stability for the future. This would satisfy the conservatives, who wanted a male ruler, and thwart Fiara, who has been waiting to assert her rule if something were to happen to me.

"Ten years ago, I finally gave birth to a son who would provide the type of stability we need. He was a joy to the court and to me, being a beautiful and happy child. Yavonne we called him. He had curly blond hair and deep brown eyes that were keenly aware. He was a special child. At the time of his birth, a prophecy came forward that this child would unite the fairy kingdoms in a century of harmony. Fiara actually appeared at court soon after the birth and mocked the prophecy, saying that it did not say when this rule would begin or that he would be alive when it was fulfilled. Our guards rushed her, but she vanished. That was the last time Fiara appeared before me. Still, we discounted her threats as mere ravings, and continued in joy for some time.

"Within a few years, while Yavonne was still small, goblins attacked our party when we were traveling through the forest and kidnapped the child. We used our strongest magic to try to locate him, but to no avail. The only trace of his whereabouts was that we knew he had made it to Fiara's cottage before disappearing. When we confronted her, she denied all. When we searched her cottage, we found no proof. In short, we know that Fiara is to blame, but we cannot convict her, and we could not find my son.

"For three years, now, we have tried to get my son back. Unfortunately, our investigations have proved fruitless. Fiara has cast a spell over her domain that prevents us from seeing into it. Because of the disappearances, few fairies are willing to approach her cottage, and anyway, her magic prevents us from approaching without being noticed. However, humans have not been under suspicion and could go there to have a better look when her guard is down. For several years, we have searched for a human child who can go to Fiara's cottage. Now, we have found you.

"This is the mission we have for you. We need you to go to Fiara's cottage to find any evidence of my son's disappearance, the attacks on my people, or any other crime. We can provide you with guidance, provisions, transportation, and anything else you want, although we cannot approach the cottage ourselves without jeopardizing your mission. Will you help us?"

Sarah thought about all that she had been taught. It was true, she had come only to rescue Lily and take her home so her mother would not worry. Sarah looked at Lily, nodding off in a chair as they had listened to the queen. As it turned out, Lily was fine, and Selena had removed the main reason for rushing back home by slowing time for her mother. The fairies had not been particularly honest at first about why they needed the girls, but that was understandable given the problems they faced—fighting discovery from humans and the witch's spies. It was not that she was angry at the fairies for taking Lily and making her worried. If Lily were to judge, she did not hold a grudge at all. Lily liked it here with the fairies. Now, the question was, what was the right thing to do?

The answer obviously was to help the fairies. Perhaps it was a motherly instinct taking over in Sarah. She could not stand the thought of that fairy child being abducted by a witch. She knew that if anything was right, it was to protect the young, whether animal or person, nice or mean. Sarah tried to imagine if someone stole one of her dolls, how much she would miss the doll. Sarah also thought about what Mommy would do if someone stole her or Lily, and what Mommy would do to get them back. Sarah needed to help Selena get the fairy child back.

Then there was also the fact that if it was a service only Sarah could provide, she had to at least try. Sarah knew that she should always try to help people, even her enemies. But somehow, she always thought that would mean just giving money. Sarah did not think she would have to go out and risk her own life. She had never done anything heroic before and was worried, as much about Lily as herself. But deep inside herself, Sarah knew what the right thing to do was, and she knew that it did not matter if people did not believe her later, or if something happened to them. She had to help even if it meant never seeing her mother again. It was the only way to save the fairies from near-disaster.

"What do you think, Lily?" Sarah asked her sister, shaking her awake.

"I want to be with the fairies," Lily said.

"Yes, I know," Sarah said, "but we would not be staying with the fairies all the time. We would have to travel a long way and face a lot of dangers. We might not get to eat big meals or wear pretty clothes, or play or sleep a lot."

"So?"

"There might be dogs."

"Doggies? Really?" Lily asked, wide-eyed, suddenly understanding the danger.

"Yes. Maybe even big ones. Maybe things worse than dogs, like goblins or witches, or mean people."

"Worse than doggies?" Lily wondered, trying to imagine something worse than a vicious dog barking loudly with pointed teeth. She looked at the queen and felt sympathy for the fairies. Lily remembered how helpless they were at the fair when the dogs attacked. "Will it help the fairies?"

"Yes."

"Maybe I could face doggies and worse if it would help other people."

Sarah sighed. "That's the way I feel, too."

Sarah knew what to do; she just needed to do it, to take a stand. Finally, she looked at the queen and blurted out, "Yes, we will help."

"Hurrah!" said Lily. "We get to go on an adventure."

5

The Witch's Cottage

By noon the following day, Sarah and Lily were on their way. They spent the morning gathering together supplies they might need—food for about a week, some extra clothes in case it started to cool, some lanterns, backpacks for each of the girls, bedrolls, a tent, elven cloaks made of a material that blended in with any background, and walking sticks. The fairies gathered and neatly packed all of the supplies for them. The old gnome worried that the packs might be too heavy for the girls, but since they were used to camping with their father, they found themselves able to easily bear the load. The girls' packs were then taken from them and strapped to their ride, a young bobwhite quail, which was waiting on top of the large tree stump where the hall was hidden.

As a final item to pack, Queen Selena gave them a potion. "When you arrive at the Fiara's cottage, you will want to return to your normal size. This potion will make you big. One mouthful will be enough. More than that will make you too big and less than that will not return you to your normal size. Use the potion sparingly, for like any drug its magic is risky and could have side-effects. Do not use it if anything gets in it or it sits too long."

As the girls packed, the queen's spies gave instructions about where they needed to go.

"The quail will take you to the barn first," a young man fairy told them. "It is less likely you will be detected that way. From the barn, go across the yard to the cottage. Unless you use the queen's potion, you need to steer clear of the farm animals. They will not likely notice you at your size, but you never can tell. Many a fairy has been swatted by a cow's tail or trampled to death by a horse because the fairy got too close to the animals without proper care. The front door of the witch's cottage enters into the main room. To the right, a door leads to the kitchen. To the left, a door leads into the bedroom. The witch's bedroom is up the stairs at the back of the main room. As far as the rest of her grounds, there is a well out front. The path from her door leads across a log bridge over a little stream, through the woods, to the nearest road. The back of her yard butts against a field, where her servants work for her growing crops. A little garden is on the side opposite of the barn. Beware the garden. That is where the witch grows her magic herbs, and these can be deadly.

"Do not try to do too much. We only want you to go and search the house for signs of the child and find out what you can about where they have taken the child. If we can just get some kind of proof, we can confront Fiara. Also, see if you can locate her wand. With the wand, she is very powerful, and knowing where the wand is will help us to avoid her using her magic. Once you have this information, return to our lands. All you need to do is make it across the bridge to the woods. Shout 'Mulberry' three times, and one of our sentries will find you and escort you back here."

"Let me add a few words of warning," Selena said. "Do not underestimate Fiara. She may look like a harmless old lady, but her magic is strong. Fiara knows many things without being told, and she has many other powers besides that of foresight. Aside from that, she is very crafty and can trick you into giving away information if she catches you. You must also look out for her servants. The men who serve her are dim-witted, but they are usually cruel and suspicious. The brownies are immature, prone to pranks, and they are not very reliable, but they can be tricky. The dark elves are as crafty as Fiara, and they have magic, too. The goblins are greedy and evil. They hate most living things. Other servants Fiara possesses are ghosts and the like, but none should be there during daylight; so, do not go near her cottage at night.

"Just go to her cottage, get the information we need, then return. Do not try to tangle with Fiara on your own. Come straight back, unless you find urgent information that requires further investigation. Do not stay more than a day or two. The longer you stay, the more likely it is she will find you. Now, go. Be blessed, and be careful," Selena said, kissing Sarah and Lily on their foreheads.

Sarah and Lily said good-bye to all the fairies they had gotten to know so well the last few hours. Selena escorted them up a secret stairway from her throne room. They climbed to the roof of the great hall where a door led out onto the top of the stump. From there, Sarah and Lily mounted the back of the quail. The fairies had built little saddles that belted on the bird's back, so they could ride more easily and safely. Once Sarah and Lily had strapped themselves in the saddles, they prepared to take off. Selena and the old gnome waved at them as the bird stood up and stepped to the edge of the stump.

The bird began to beat its wings, blowing dust up. Warning Sarah and Lily about the dust, the fairies had given them bandanas to wrap around their mouths and noses. The bird flew up above the stump, folded its legs, and flew out over their yard. The girls could see the stump in the tree line at the back of the yard grow smaller and smaller. As they flew up over the house, they could see the roof and leaves falling on it. The quail circled around and started to fly south. Soon, the girls were up high enough they could see their street with cars moving on it, their neighborhood, and all the familiar trees and landmarks: the school down the street, the church at the end of the road, and the playground. Lily kept yelling out and pointing whenever she saw someplace she knew.

After the girls gained enough altitude, they really started moving. It was not until then that Lily began to get nervous about how high they were. Sarah had always enjoyed roller coasters or other amusement rides, so she was not really fazed by it. But Sarah knew that Lily never was one to enjoy that kind of thrill. Sarah tried to distract Lily by pointing out places they knew in other parts of the city that Lily might not recognize: the mall where they shopped, the road to their grandmother's house, and the park. After a while, Lily realized that they were safely strapped in and began to enjoy the ride.

As the girls increased speed, the wind was blowing through their hair and in their faces. It was like being on a swing, only you were always going forward. Up there in the sky, the sun was constantly beating on them, so the girls did not get as cold as you might imagine. At one point, they flew through a low cloud that did make them cold. The sun disappeared for a moment, and all around was fluffy white. As they emerged from the clouds, the girls noticed that they were covered with water, which took a few minutes to dry off. Now when they looked down, everything seemed so far off, like looking at a map. It was easy to forget how high they were because they could not make out people and cars. All the girls could see were neighborhoods like little blocks, wide furrowed fields like corduroy patches, green wooded areas, and the river winding like a blue thread.

Finally, after the girls crossed the river, they began to go down again. In neat little circles, they flew closer and closer to the ground until they could make out the individual trees, a road, and some houses. As they dipped, Lily pointed to the right. There was a little cottage next to a field with a well in the front and a barn on one side. It was the witch's cottage. The momentary enjoyment of the ride began to fade as the girls remembered what they were there to do and the danger that they faced.

The quail continued to circle around, getting lower and lower, until it flew into a window at the top of the barn. The girls landed on a large, soft bale of hay. The quail settled down on its belly, letting them get off easier. Sarah unbuckled Lily and held her hand as she slid to the ground. Then Sarah threw off their packs and other supplies and slid off the bird herself.

"Thank you very much for the ride," Sarah said to the bird. "We really enjoyed it. You were very safe. Now, we have to go into the witch's house. It will probably be dangerous, so go on back to the fairies. We will be all right from here."

The bird cooed, then it got up and flew up to the windowsill at the top of the barn and looked back at the girls.

"It's OK," Sarah reiterated. "Tell the queen we will meet her people in the woods."

The bird flew off as Sarah and Lily began to look around at their surroundings. They were in the hayloft of the barn. Behind them was a mountain of hay. Just to their left, directly in front of the window, was an opening in the floor leading to the barn. The girls looked around for a way to get down. There was a ladder going down, but they now realized that the ladder rungs were too far apart for them to reach.

"Why don't you make us big, now?" said Lily. "Then we could reach the ladder."

"I don't know," said Sarah. "I was thinking that maybe it would be better to wait. After all, we are going into the witch's house. If we are big, she might find us easier. If we stay little, we could sneak around better, and the witch might not be able to see us. I mean, the only advantage of being big is that we could run faster, maybe fight better, and get people's attention. We really need stealth more than strength, at least until we search the house and are ready to get away. Then we can make ourselves big."

"Well, how are we going to reach the ladder?" Lily asked.

Sarah looked through her things. "I have Daddy's rope," she said hopefully. Sarah was glad now that she had packed it because the fairies had not given her one. Luckily, it had shrunk when they did, so it was just the right size. She unrolled it. It was just long enough to make it down to the first rung. Sarah looked around and found a nail she could attach it to; on the rung below she saw another nail. She made a loop in the rope, put it around the nail next to them, and then she lowered the rope down. First, Sarah climbed down, and next Lily came down far enough for Sarah to catch her. Then Sarah wiggled the rope until it came undone from the nail. Attaching the rope to the nail on that rung of the latter on which they now stood, they climbed down to the next step. On that rung, the girls found a large splinter sticking out to which they could attach the rope, and they climbed down to the next step. In a few hours of hard work, they made it down to the floor of the barn. Looking up at the ladder, the girls were amazed—it was like they had been cliff climbing, something they would never have done in real life. Somehow being smaller made it seem easier since they were just climbing down a ladder.

Sarah had been careful to look around while they were climbing down and knew that there were no animals in the barn, at least at that time. A pen next to the barn held some horses, and there was a pigsty on the other side of the pen. Probably, the animals came into the barn at night. At least for now, though, there was no danger of animals.

"Maybe we should look around the barn, first," Lily said.

"There's just hay in here," Sarah replied. "We are supposed to search the cottage."

"If *I* were going to hide something, I would either keep it in a secret place in my room or else I would put it out of the house, maybe in the garage."

"Perhaps you are right," Sarah said. "Let's nose around here."

Sarah and Lily collected their packs and started searching around the barn. They looked under the hay, in the stalls, and under the manger. At one point, they did find a door, which was locked by a padlock. The girls could crack the door, but only enough to look in, not enough to squeeze through. Looking inside the room, they saw what appeared to be a storeroom. Above them a cracked window provided light. Within view of the door there were stacks of fertilizer, a bucket, a shovel, a pitchfork, and an old pair of boots—what you would expect to find in a barn storeroom. They could see nothing suspicious. Still, Sarah made a mental picture of the place, noting that if they ever needed to come back, they could probably crawl through a chipped corner of one windowpane.

"Come on," Sarah said, "We need to start making for the cottage. It will be dark soon."

The girls adjusted their packs and made it across the barn to the heavy door. Suddenly, Sarah realized that they would not be able to open the extremely heavy door, and she did not see a way under it. They would have to make it out through the horse pen. An entrance on one side of the barn opened into the pen, and the fence surrounding the pen was built into the barn wall. In order to get out under the fence, the girls would have to risk going under the horse's feet. It would be dangerous since the horse could step on them at any time. It was a risk they would have to take since that was the only way out.

"It's getting dark in here," Lily said.

"Yes, it will be night soon," Sarah said.

"I'm scared to go out in the yard at night. There could be monsters. Isn't that what the fairies said?"

"Yes, you are probably right. Maybe we could camp in here tonight and make it out into the yard first thing in the morning."

They agreed and looked around for a place to sleep. Lily suggested lying in the hay in the manger, but Sarah was worried that a horse might come in and eat them with the hay. So they found a spot in a corner of one unused stall to pitch their tent. Although the tent was different from the ones they used when camping with their father, the girls soon figured it out and set up the tent.

"Can we start a fire?" Lily asked.

"I don't think we should risk it. It would attract anyone that comes in the barn. It should be warm enough in here, and I have my flashlight if we need light," Sarah said.

Sarah and Lily went ahead and settled into the tent pulling out some of the food the fairies packed for them. There were some nuts and berries, all unusually large. Of course, Sarah knew at once this was because they were so small. There was also bread made of some kind of grain and honey with a nice grassy smell, which was surprisingly good. The girls washed it all down with a drink made of dew flavored with honey, also very good. After they ate, they lay down and went to sleep. Feeling so safe and secure in the warm barn, and so trusting were they, the girls slept straight through until morning without a guard, without a worry.

The next day, Sarah and Lily broke camp, packed up, and set out for the cottage at last. As they had decided the previous evening, the girls went under the fence into the horse pen, so they could cut back under the fence to the outside of the barn. There was a horse standing in the corner right where they needed to go, a big white horse with brown spots. Trying to make the least amount of noise they could, the girls started walking straight under the horse toward the outer fence. They had not taken more than thirty or forty steps when the horse started shuffling his feet. At one point, he lifted a foot and put it down only inches behind where Lily was walking. This gave Lily a scare, and she started to run! Sarah followed closely behind her, hoping the horse would not come any closer. In a few minutes the girls were under the fence surrounding the pen and out in the yard.

"That was close," Sarah said. Lily nodded in agreement as she tried to catch her breath.

The girls looked across the barnyard to the cottage. They could see where the path from the front door led out, past a well, and off toward the woods where they knew the log bridge was waiting, although they could not see it. The cottage looked ordinary enough and seemed clean and well kempt. It was not at all what they expected from a witch's cottage. From the descriptions of Fiara, they thought it would be dark, ugly, and full of dust and spider webs. The house they saw was pretty and kind of cute. The outside was freshly whitewashed, the thatched roof appeared in good repair, and the Dutch door and shutters on the three windows—two downstairs and one upstairs—were painted emerald green. Smoke curled gently from the chimney. Sarah wondered whether the neat and clean appearance of the cottage was because the witch used her magic to appear friendly and nice, not evil. It always seemed to Sarah that things that were truly evil always looked fair on the outside and were not black or hideous. Good people, as often as not, were ugly or at least not always pretty.

Sarah and Lily started to make their way across the yard. Now that they were nearing the dangerous part of the mission, they found themselves being a little more cautious. Somehow, it seemed like someone was watching them. They felt a little uncomfortable being out in the open, so they took the hundred feet or so to the cottage in stages, trying to stay behind cover as much as possible. First, the girls moved along the edge of the fence, on the outside so as to avoid the animals penned up, until the fence ran into the pigsty. Next, they cut across an open spot to a wagon that was more or less in the center of the yard, trying to hide behind rocks and grass when they could. After watching the house for some time and seeing no one going in or out, the girls ran from behind a wagon wheel to the flowerbed next to the house. Hiding under the crabgrass lining the flower beds, they moved along the side of the house until they reached the door.

Sarah and Lily finally made it to their destination, but they found once again that the door was shut and that they could not fit under it. This time, however, Sarah had planned it out. Moving to the end of the building where a water drain came down from the roof, the girls pulled themselves up on the bracket fairly easily, and from there, they could reach a window box where some pansies were growing. From there, they were able to get on the windowsill and push their way through a window that was slightly ajar. It took them several minutes, but finally, Sarah and Lily were inside the witch's cottage!

6

At Home

Sarah and Lily stood on the windowsill for some time, trying to scope out the witch's home. The cottage was dark, so it took a few minutes for their eyes to adjust to the shade. Observing the living room of the cottage, the girls saw two chairs, a spinning wheel in a corner, an unlit lamp hanging from the ceiling, and a fireplace with glowing embers left from the last fire. A large wooden mantle ran across the top, with a clock in the middle. Next to the mantle was an opening that led to the kitchen. The girls could just make out a sink on the far wall. To their left was a cracked door leading into a bedroom or storage room. In front of them and just past the door was a stairway leading to the loft above them. There, according to the intelligence they received from the fairies, was where the witch stayed. Nothing moved, not even a breeze. If it were not for the fire, Sarah and Lily would have said the place was deserted.

"It looks like no one is home," Sarah whispered to Lily. Lily nodded. "Where should we start?" Sarah added quietly.

"Let's start with the guest room. Maybe she is keeping the baby in there."

Sarah nodded. They moved to some drapes hanging near the window and found that the stitches in the fabric were just far enough apart that it made an almost perfect rope ladder. They climbed quickly down to the hard wood floor and moved silently across it to the door and into the next room. It was a plain room with a bed, a dresser, and a door on the right leading into the bathroom. The bed was neatly made with a large quilt.

Sarah and Lily walked over to the bathroom first. Inside were a tub, a sink, and a toilet. Sarah was amazed that the rustic cottage had indoor plumbing. It seemed an odd mixture of old and new. In front of the sink was an ordinary mirror. Nothing seemed out of place in the room. Still, they thought they should at least look in the tub and sink, so they climbed up a towel hanging on the edge of the tub. The tub was empty. From the edge of the tub, they could just see into the sink using the mirror, and it appeared empty as well.

"Nothing in here," Sarah said.

The girls walked back in the bedroom in front of the chest of drawers. The drawers were all shut, with handles an arm's length apart.

"How do we get up there to check in the drawers?" Lily asked.

"Hmm," Sarah wondered. "Being fairy-size isn't all it's cracked up to be. Maybe if we had their wings and could fly, it would not be that bad. Well, I suppose we will need to be big to look in those unless we can get someone else to open them. Why don't we save that for last and finish looking around instead."

Lily agreed, so they left and walked over to the kitchen. Once again, they found it resembled an ordinary kitchen. There was a kitchen table with three stools around it. An iron stove was on one side, and a china cabinet was on the other. The sink was set in a cabinet with doors. With a great deal of effort, they used Sarah's rope to pull one of the cabinet doors open. Inside were a garbage can and some cleaning bottles, just what you would expect. The girls turned to leave and saw a black iron cauldron hanging over the fire.

"Maybe she has some potion brewing," Sarah said. They carefully drew closer.

"Smells more like stew," said Lily.

The one place the girls still had not searched was the witch's room. It was with great reluctance that they decided to head up the stairs. Luckily, the steps were close together, like they were made for someone short in stature. The girls were able to reach from step to step. In half an hour, they had climbed the steps and now faced the door to the witch's room. It was not all the way shut, so the girls were able to push it open.

Sarah and Lily walked quietly inside. The room was dark, even darker than the rest of the house. Heavy curtains blocked all light coming in from the windows. The only light seemed to come from the doorway behind them. Still, they could see a bed, a bookshelf with lots of old books, a wardrobe, and chest of drawers with a mirror. The bed was unmade, and they could hear a soft snoring noise coming from the bed. Quietly, they walked over to the bookshelf and started to climb up so they could get a better view.

Once Sarah and Lily made it up to the third shelf, they looked out again over the room. They could see the sleeping form of an old lady on the bed. Queen Selena was right—she looked quite harmless, but because of the warning, the girls were not fooled. They could see the wardrobe partly open. Inside there were some clothes hanging, but they could see little else. Once again, Sarah and Lily saw no sign of the fairy child.

Sarah turned and looked at the books, hoping for some sign of the fairy child or other crimes the witch had committed. There were some history books, including a history of brownies, some books on farming, and even an atlas. There were also a lot of magic books with titles such as *Potions and Cures*, *How to Bewitch Humans*, and *The Art of Transformation*. The latter seemed particularly interesting. Maybe the witch turned the fairy child and all the missing fairies into something else. Sarah tried pulling the book out, but it was too heavy. Lily went around to the back of the books and helped push on the book until finally it began to move, but the girls moved it so fast it fell off the shelf, landing open, face up on the floor. They climbed down and then crawled on top of the book as Sarah tried to read a few pages. It was very difficult because she had to stand on the page to read it, and the pages were very large and heavy, so that she had to climb off to turn them.

Sarah glanced over the table of contents, which she learned in school was where you could get the best idea of what is in a book. There were spells for changing people into animals, animals into monsters, and even living creatures into stone. Sarah flipped the pages to look at a few. Lily looked over Sarah's shoulder, but most of the pages were all words. Only a few had pictures, which were drawings. Each page read like a recipe—there were measurements and requirements at the top, and instructions how to make it work at the bottom. Most of the spells she looked at required a wand; some required potions with weird ingredients like "1 cup bat wings" or "1 tsp of arsenic." Some required boiling ingredients while concentrating on your victim, burying objects beneath the full moon, or applying salves while saying magic words. Unfortunately, most of the words of the incantations were in a language Sarah did not know, so she could not understand the words.

As Sarah and Lily looked intently at the book, they suddenly heard a purring noise that was as loud to them as a lion's roar. A cat was peering down from the edge of the bed. Apparently, the falling book had woken it up from where it was sleeping next to the witch. However, the witch still did not stir, so at first, they thought it was safe.

"Nice kitty," Lily said, starting to walk toward the animal.

"Lily, I'm not sure it's a nice kitty. In fact, it's looking at us like it is hungry."

And the cat was looking at Sarah and Lily, sort of licking its lips as you might lick your lips when your mother puts your favorite dessert in front of you.

"Maybe it thinks we are mice," Lily responded. "I mean, we are about the same size as mice."

The girls looked at each other and realized that Lily had stumbled onto the truth. They did look a lot like mice, but it was not just their size. Their hoodies could have been ears, and the rope Sarah was dragging behind her looked like a tail. They may have even smelled like mice because of all the field mice, rabbits, or other rodents that were always around the fairies.

"Start to back up toward the door," Sarah said, "but do it calmly without any sudden movements."

As the girls backed up slowly, the cat's eyes followed them. Moving to the corner of the bed nearest the door, the cat reared back like it was about to pounce. At that moment, Sarah and Lily bolted toward the door. In an instant, the cat was on the floor running toward them. Sarah made it out the door first, and immediately she started to push on the door. It was too heavy, so she put her back against it and braced her feet on the ground. It started to budge. Just as Lily ran through the crack, Sarah got the door mostly closed, trapping the cat in the room.

Sarah and Lily ran to the steps and began to slide down them as quickly as they could. About the time they were halfway down, the girls saw the door open and knew that the cat was in hot pursuit. Another moment later and another step down, they saw the cat's head look over the top step. In another few seconds, the cat would be on top of them. Sarah looked down. Directly below them was the spinning wheel. Next to the spinning wheel was a basket containing different colored yarn. It was only a few feet down, although at their size it was more like a cliff or tall building, and the basket was like a large pool.

"Quick, Lily, jump into the yarn."

Sarah jumped first and landed softly in the yarn. She waved to Lily to jump next. Sarah could see the cat running down the stairs toward her sister. Now, Sarah was not particularly athletic, but she tended to be fearless. She was not scared of heights and loved rides and thrills, but Lily was different. Lily was always a little bit afraid of high places. Ever since she fell down the stairs when she was young, Lily was always a little extra careful, and cliffs were out of the question. But Lily was more scared of the cat, which was roaring down the stairs toward her. It was about the bravest thing she had done in her life, but Lily closed her eyes and jumped off, hoping that Sarah would catch her. She, too, landed in the yarn. Quickly, the girls covered themselves up, hoping that they could hide.

The cat ran down the stairs. The girls heard it run into the kitchen, and then they heard it walking around the chairs. Obviously, the cat was looking for them.

"We'll never get away," Sarah whispered, "at least not while that cat is looking for us. If only we could get rid of it long enough to get out of the house."

The girls looked around at the yarn and out toward the chair, where the cat was perched on the arm scanning the floor for the children.

"Say," Lily said, "don't kitty cats like playing with balls of yarn?"

"Yes," Sarah answered. "Yeah," she said slower, when she understood what was Lily was suggesting.

"Here, hand me the end of that ball of yarn," Sarah said. Lily handed her a long strand of yard coming off a ball of red yarn. Sarah took the end and tied it around the handle of the basket, which was just within reach.

"OK, now help me lift up the ball of yarn."

Sarah and Lily both got under the ball and started to lift it up. It looked enormous compared to them, so they assumed it would be heavy, but it was feather light. Pushing the ball of yarn up and over the edge of the basket, the girls watched it roll out of the basket, hit the floor, unwind across the floor, and roll straight through the open door of the guest bedroom.

"Perfect," Sarah said. "Now, get ready to run."

The cat leapt down, and drawn like a baby to a toy, it took off after the ball of yarn, batting at it as a little kitten might, and chasing it as it rolled.

"Never fails," Sarah said. "Now, quick, over the edge and run back toward the window while the cat is distracted."

All the girls had to do was to make it to the windowsill. The cat could not reach that high and would take several minutes to get up to them. By that time, they could make it out the window and hide in the garden. If the cat continued to pursue them, there were plenty of places to hide.

Unfortunately, they had no such luck. As soon as the cat caught up with the ball of yarn and had it in its paws, it realized it had been tricked. That's when it looked back and saw the two tiny figures running across the middle of the floor. As quick as a wink, the cat was through the door and after the girls.

Sarah and Lily had just made it to the curtain when the cat came running into the room. Sarah knew that they did not have a chance to make it up the curtain, but she thought perhaps she could distract the cat while Lily did.

"Keep going, Lily. I will keep the cat busy."

"No," Lily said. "I want to be with you."

So they both ran under a brown arm chair. The cat, however, could not stop in time and ran into the chair head first. The chair was too low to the ground for the cat to run under it, but it could crawl slowly under the chair, so it crouched down, wiggled under the chair, and started to reach for the children, who backed toward the wall.

By the time the cat was finally within reach, Sarah and Lily made it to the other side of the chair. The cat would soon be out, too. The only place to run was a little hole in the wainscot that was just the right size for them. The cat would not be able to follow, although the hole was large enough for it to reach inside. Quickly, the girls bolted toward the hole, and just made it inside when the cat grabbed at them from behind, missing them by inches.

It was pitch black in the hole, and it took a few minutes for the girls' eyes to adjust well enough for them to make out a passage along the edge of the wall to their right. They ran down the passage just in time—the cat had begun to paw around the inside of the hole. The girls heard its meow booming through the hole, amplified into a terrible noise that echoed down the tunnel. In the light coming from the hole, they saw the cat reach as far as it could after them, but it still came up short several inches. Sarah and Lily were safe.

"Well, now all we have to do is wait for the cat to leave or find another way out," Sarah said. "I suppose we should look for an exit."

"I wonder what lives in this hole?" Lily asked. Neither one had given much thought to the idea because they just wanted to get away from the cat. Now it dawned on them that something made that hole—a bug, a rat, or maybe a snake?

Sarah and Lily started to walk away from the cat's paws and deeper into the hole, but blocking the passage ahead of them was a furry shape. They quietly moved to one side of the passage. When the light shining past them hit the shape, the girls saw that it was a giant mouse with a red light gleaming in its eyes. This time, they were caught. Sarah and Lily could not go forward because the mouse blocked the way, and they could not go back into the cat's paws. The girls stalled for several minutes, staying as still as possible, hoping beyond hope that the mouse would not see them. But the giant mouse began to advance toward them until it stopped right in front of them. A red light gleamed in its eyes. The mouse stood up on its back legs, towering some nine inches tall, ready to lunge at Sarah and Lily.

7

In the Mouse Hole

The mouse advanced toward Sarah and Lily, but instead of attacking them, it held out its paw as if in friendship.

"Please do not be scared," the mouse said.

"It can talk!" Lily exclaimed.

"Of course," the mouse replied.

Then Lily noticed that on its head was a circlet of gold.

"Look, Sarah," said Lily, "It's wearing a headband. Maybe it is not a real mouse."

"That is very observant," said the mouse. "In fact, I am an elf that the witch transformed into a mouse. As you can probably guess, I am no ally of the witch, so I can be trusted. If you will follow me, I will take you away from the cat. I have had to deal with him many times."

The mouse started to scurry down a long straight passage along the edge of the wall. Sarah was not sure whether to trust the mouse or not, but seeing that the only other alternative was to try to leave the hole and brave the cat, she decided to play along. Lily, meanwhile, had caught up to the mouse and was asking it all kinds of questions.

"Where are you taking us?"

"To a safe place where we can talk. I have a nice hole near here. It is a bit of a walk, but once we get there, we can talk at leisure."

"How did the witch turn you into a mouse?"

"She used her magic wand."

"How long have you been a mouse?"

"Oh, about a year now."

"Why didn't you run away?"

"I did at first, but none of my own people were able to help. I realized that the only way to get changed back was to get the witch to do it. So I have been hanging around here looking for an opportunity."

"I thought the elves were the witch's friends," Sarah interjected, now catching up.

"Some of my people are, but it is mostly the dark elves. You see, there are many different groups of elves. There are the sylvan or woodland elves, who are smaller and very frivolous. Then there are the high elves, of which I am one. We come from the oldest families and tend to be more serious, and therefore are the chieftains and leaders. We are also in stature closer to men. Then there are the dark elves, who tend toward mischief. It is said that long ago, they fell under the influence of the enemy. Many live in caves or come out only at night. A few continue to commune with the other elves, but they are still very independent, frequently work with men or goblins, and have a cruel streak. These are the elves that supported the witch, probably because they felt that they would benefit from her rule."

Making a turn through a hole cut in the wooden frame, the girls saw a large round door made from a knot in the wood. In the center of the door was a handle, by which the mouse opened it.

"I put in doors every so often along the passageway. It keeps out a lot of creatures I don't want to follow me, like real rats and mice."

Once the girls and the mouse passed through the door, they went down another passage and made a sharp turn to the right. They continued on for a short way until they came to what appeared to be a small pool blocking the path. A series of steps made from nails stuck in the wall went up like a ladder. At the top of the stairs was a pipe running parallel to the wall, which formed a little path. It sloped off each side, and there was a long drop into the darkness below. The wall was just outside of arm's length on one side. They climbed carefully up and stepped out onto the pipe.

"Make sure to walk down the middle of the pipe," the mouse instructed the girls. "It gets slippery, which makes it easy to slide off the edges. If you slip, try to fall toward the wall so you can catch yourself."

As they walked in single file for another few feet, they came to another set of nails going down. Once down, the passage continued ahead.

"Why did we go up on the pipe and back down?" Lily asked.

"The pool we passed runs several feet inside the walls. You can just see it behind us," the mouse replied. They looked back and could just see the edge of a pool of water.

"Where did the pool come from?" Sarah asked.

"One of the pipes started to leak a few months ago. The witch probably will not notice until it rots a hole in the wall. Anyway, I had to create a passageway to get over it."

The girls followed the mouse along the passage for several more feet, passing through two holes in the studs and making another turn to the right. The passageway dead-ended into another door. On the other side was a little chamber formed by two planks coming together. The mouse went in front of them, and on the floor was a hole plugged by what appeared to be a drain stopper with a large handle in the middle. The mouse pulled on the plug, opening the trap door. There were steps formed of mortar leading down between two rocks. The girls walked down the stairs and ended in a little two-room apartment made from one of the cinder blocks that formed the foundation of the cottage.

"This is my home," the mouse said. "Please make yourself comfortable. Now, forgive me. Where are my manners? We did not have time for proper introductions while running from the cat. My name is Elwin."

"My name is Sarah, and this is my sister Lily."

"Pleased to meet you," the mouse said, shaking their hands. His hands were leathery but rather soft and gentle.

They went inside and shut the door. There was a smooth table formed of bathroom tile in the middle of the room sitting on a bit of brick, and chairs made of old wooden spools surrounded it. On the wall was a picture of a Christmas tree made of a postage stamp framed by bits of a popsicle stick, and in the corner was a stove made of some old metal car part that was hollow in the middle. A piece of pipe made from an ink pen ran out the back and up through the wall. Elwin threw some twigs into the stove, pulled out a match as long as his arm, struck it on the wall, and threw it onto the fire. Soon, it was bright and cozy in the room. Then he went to an old matchbox, which he used as a drawer, and pulled out some morsel of food. He scurried about pulling out pots and pans made from bottle caps, a thimble, and a rounded penny, and he started preparing the food. As Elwin busied himself, he regaled them with stories of how he had outwitted the cat. Soon Sarah and Lily were sitting with the mouse eating and talking.

"You have a very nice house," Lily said. It was cozy, but rather plain. Still, Mommy had always said to be polite to strangers, especially when you are visiting their house, and Lily thought this probably applied to mice as well.

"Thank you," said Elwin. "I do what I can."

"It is a fantastic set of tunnels you have built here," Sarah said.

"Yes, I have tunnels leading to every room and even to spots out in the yard."

"It must have taken you a long time to build them."

"Yes, several months of hard work, but that was the only way I could keep tabs on the witch. Besides, what else was I to do with my time?"

"So what exactly is your story?" Sarah asked.

"My story is rather simple," the mouse said. "My sister, Elaura, strayed too near the witch's house about a year ago and disappeared. I came to look for her, but she was not to be found. I did discover that the witch had a wand that turned people into things, and I tried to steal it. When the witch found out, she turned me into a mouse and set her cat on me. I was able to jab the cat with a pin I had been wearing, and then I escaped inside the wall. After about a week, I escaped across the fields and found some elves. The older of them, who was well versed in magic, said that they could not undo the witch's magic without her wand."

"Was he a magician?" Sarah asked.

"He was not a magician in the same way that some humans are, but all elves have powers that I suppose some people would call magic. Some have definite gifts—healing, concealment, or even second sight. However, because they grow up around it, even the simplest of elves have what big people might call a magical quality, the ability to move quietly, see in the dark, and so forth. It just seems magical to non-elves.

"Anyway, they said they would try to help by carrying a message back to our people. I never saw or heard from them again. I assume the witch got to them because no one ever came. Instead, I returned to the house to try to spy on the witch and look for an opportunity to get that wand and either turn myself back somehow or get it to the fairy folk."

By this time, the girls had finished eating, and the mouse took out a pipe carved of wood, pulled out a pouch from a drawer, removed a brand from the fire to light it, and started puffing away. The girls looked at him with wonder.

"Oh, I stole the tobacco from an old cigar that one of the humans dropped," he said to their questioning looks. "It really would be uncivilized to go without a good smoke after dinner."

Elwin puffed away for a moment or two, sending large billowing smoke rings into a corner of the ceiling.

"And what of yourselves? What brings two little girls the size of mice into a witch's home?"

"We were chosen by the Fairy Queen to find her child. She said because of the fairies disappearing near the witch's home, she needed human children to come who would not be detected by the witch's magic," Sarah said.

"Say," she continued, "You have been watching the witch for a year. Have you heard her say anything about the fairy child?"

"No, I'm afraid not. But that would have happened long before I came here. Of course, she has captured many fairies since I have been here. A few she has kept alive in cages until their usefulness was gone. The truly dangerous ones she turned to mice or birds to feed to her cat. If she felt like she might need them again, she turned them to stones or flightless creatures and took them to Crow Island."

"Where is this cage?" Sarah asked.

"It is in her room, hanging from the ceiling," Elwin said. "But it is empty right now. In fact, she has not kept anyone there for many weeks, and she never keeps them more than a day or so."

"What about the island? Is it far from here?" Sarah asked.

"It is several miles away, in the middle of a lake. But at our size, it would seem much farther. Most of the way to the lake lies within the witch's lands, making it very dangerous."

"Well, we can stay here and watch the witch, or go to the island to check it out. Since you have watched the witch for months and not seen or heard about the fairy child, it seems like the island is the best place to continue our search. Do you think you could show us the way?" Sarah asked.

"Certainly," Elwin said. "But, as I said, it is a long journey fraught with danger. We will have to pass near the whispering pines, avoid goblin patrols, outwit brownies, and figure out a way to get across the lake. If the witch's servants find out about us, they would pursue us and try to capture us. But the worst danger is getting away from this house. That cat watches the yard like a hawk, and the longer you stay, the more likely it is the witch will learn of your presence."

"If we are going to complete the mission we accepted," Sarah said, "we really have no choice but to go."

"All right, but we will need to get a good night's rest. Why don't you two stay in my room. I will keep watch out here. Then tomorrow, we can plan and pack."

The girls agreed. After sitting up a few more hours talking, telling stories, and snacking, they all started to tire. Sarah and Lily went into the mouse's room and found his bed, which was a box containing some cotton and covered with an old hanky—neatly washed. They settled in and found it particularly warm and cozy. Soon, they drifted off to sleep. That night, Sarah dreamed of the fairy child playing in a garden somewhere, flying around and playing hide-and-go-seek with the bees and butterflies. She woke up and wondered whether she had second sight and her dream would come to pass. Would they be able to find the fairy child? Even if they found him, could they save him? Sarah looked at Lily sleeping peacefully. She could not bear the thought of someone kidnapping Lily. How much more did Selena wish to save her son? She knew then that they made the right decision to help the fairies. She rolled over and went back to sleep. Lily, meanwhile, dreamed of hugging the soft little mouse and stroking its fur, which is what she wanted to do all along.

8

The Whispering Pines

After waking refreshed, Sarah, Lily, and the mouse Elwin washed in a basin made of a bit of chipped porcelain filled with water leaking from a pipe. They dried their faces on a towel made of an old cut up dishrag. After a short breakfast, they packed some food and supplies, got their packs together, and left the house behind them. Elwin took them through several winding passages and up a flight of rough stairs carved into the mortar until they came to a crack between two bricks. If they turned sideways and breathed in deeply, taking off their packs, they could just barely fit through. On the other side was a wide tunnel carved into wood. It went straight ahead for two or three feet and ended at a round door.

Elwin worked the latch and opened the door, and Sarah and Lily saw they were at a great height (well, four or five feet, which seemed great to them). They all stood near the top of a woodpile on the edge of a piece of firewood. The tunnel bored through the middle of one of the logs. The door was very cleverly disguised to look like the end of the log. About a dozen yards away, across the farmyard, they could see some trees.

"This door is the closest one to the woods. We should be able to make it across the yard and find cover there, provided we can distract the cat, as we discussed," Elwin said. "The cat is always in the yard this time of day and chases mice and other rodents."

"If there was something else the cat could chase, that would distract it, wouldn't it?" Sarah said.

"A decoy. Yes, that would work, but the question is, what could we use as a decoy?" Elwin asked.

Sarah could not think of anything, at least anything that they could control. "Maybe if we used something else as bait. Like food."

"Yes, and we have food," said Elwin. "I have some ham that the cat would like, but it's only a little. I'm not sure it is enough to interest him. If only we had something really big."

"Why don't we use the potion to make your ham big?" Lily asked.

"Potion? What potion?" Elwin asked.

"The Fairy Queen gave us a potion to return us to our normal height. That's a good idea, Lily. We can use the potion to make the ham big. Now, where should we leave it?" Sarah asked.

"I would leave it over by the well," said Elwin. "It's on the other side of the house, so it will keep him out of sight when he finds it. All we have to do is walk around the edge of the house, so we are not seen."

"I will go with you with the potion," Sarah said. "Lily, can you wait here until we get back? Since we can run faster, it would be safer if you stay."

"OK," she said. "But don't be too long."

"Now don't wander off or touch anything. Just wait here for us, and we'll be right back. Then we can run from here to the wood."

Lily watched Sarah and Elwin climb down from the woodpile and move to the right along the edge of the cottage until they crept around the corner. She waited for several minutes, enough time for them to have made it to the well. Then she saw the cat walk around the opposite side of the house to her left. She watched as the cat sniffed around and guessed that it had detected the mouse's scent. She wanted to call out to warn them, but she realized that if she did the cat would come after her. So she waited breathlessly, hoping that Sarah and Elwin had hidden themselves or that the cat would be distracted just long enough. The cat rounded the corner to her right where Sarah and Elwin had gone. She heard the cat screech and feared the worst. Five minutes passed, then ten minutes. She was just about to give up and call out when Sarah and Elwin came around the opposite side of the house to her left, the side from where the cat had originally come. They motioned to Lily, and she climbed down from the woodpile, using the logs as steps and ledges.

"What happened?" Lily asked when she caught up with them.

"In a minute," Elwin said. "Let's get out of sight."

They ran across the field and into the tree line. They kept running for some time until the underbrush was thick enough to hide them. Then they stopped behind a bush to catch their breath. Sarah brought Lily up to date.

"We had just put the ham out and poured a drop of the potion on it—boy, did that work. It grew really big—taller than a house, at least at our size. Anyway, we had just put it out when the cat came around the corner. We hid behind the well, and the cat ran straight for the ham in glee. It was so busy gorging itself that we ran around the other side of the house without it noticing."

"Well, is everyone rested?" Elwin asked. The girls nodded. "We had better put some distance between us and the cottage, then. Let's get moving."

Sarah, Lily, and Elwin each picked out a good walking stick from twigs and sticks lying beneath the bushes and then set off to the lake. They continued through thick bushes for some time before finally breaking out into an area of the forest where the trees were spread farther apart, allowing them to walk side by side comfortably. After about an hour of walking, they noticed that the hearty oaks, maples, poplars, and elms were giving way more and more to pine. After another few minutes of walking, the trees were all pine—tall, North Georgia pines with almost no underbrush and with branches many feet over their heads. As far as they could see, there was row after row of straight pines stretching into the distance, lined up like the columns in some outdoor hall. It appeared to be a part of the forest that was very little traveled, for there were no paths, and the floor of the forest was an undisturbed bed of orange and brown pine needles. The needles cushioned every footstep, so that it became very quiet, deathly quiet in fact. There were no leaves crunching, no animals heard scurrying about, and no birds flying except so far overhead they were only echoes. The only sound was the slight whispering of the wind through the pine needles and the faint pad of their footsteps.

The three continued walking on in silence—it seemed sacrilege somehow to break the stillness of that wilderness cathedral by talking. With very little shade, the sun was shining brightly on them. After a time, with the air seeming particularly still and warm, the needles beneath their feet so soft, the company so pleasant, and the place so quiet, each of them began to feel very tired.

"I'm sleepy," Lily said.

"Let's stop for a rest," Sarah added.

At first, Elwin looked as though he were going to agree. Then he abruptly said, "No, we have not gone that far. You girls are too soft and can't keep up."

"What do you mean we can't keep up?" Sarah said.

"Just what I said," repeated Elwin. "Girls are soft and can't keep up with boys."

"But we are keeping up just fine," Sarah blurted.

"Yes, we are used to hiking with Daddy," Lily said.

"Anyway," Sarah added, "at least we plan better. You would not have packed nearly enough food if it weren't for us."

"Yeah! Girls are better than boys," Lily added.

"How do you figure?" Elwin asked.

"Because girls are prettier, cleaner, neater, and sweeter," Sarah said.

"Says who?" Elwin said.

"Everyone knows it. It's just like the rhyme our Daddy used to say to us."

"What rhyme?"

Lily stopped briefly and began to recite:

What are little girls made of?
What are little girls made of?
Sugar and spice and everything nice.
That's what little girls are made of.

What are little boys made of?
What are little boys made of?
Frogs and snails and puppy dog tails.
That's what little boys are made of.

"That's not how it goes," Elwin said.

"Is so!" Lily and Sarah said together, starting to walk again.

"Is not!" he replied.

"Well then, how does it go?" Sarah asked mocking.

Elwin began to say:

What are little mice made of?
What are little mice made of?
Cheese and fleas and thank you's please.
That's what little mice are made of.

What are human beings made of?
What are human beings made of?
Noise and toys and mean little boys.
That's what human beings are made of.

"I've never heard it that way before," Lily said.

"That wouldn't surprise me. You have not been around long enough to know a lot."

"Well, I haven't heard it either. In fact, that was the most ridiculous nursery rhyme I've ever heard," Sarah said. "Besides, look at what it says—little BOYS are mean. Not little girls. Everyone knows that we are quiet and nice."

"Ah, but look at the witch. Isn't she a girl?"

"Well, sort of . . ." Sarah began.

"She's an elf," Lily finished.

"That's right," Sarah came back, "She's not really a girl because she's not human."

"But she is a girl elf, is she not?" Elwin asked.

"It's not the same thing," Sarah said. "She's all of the things that real ladies aren't."

"And just who told you what real ladies are?" Elwin asked.

"My mother!" Sarah exclaimed.

"And what does your mother know about it?"

"First of all, don't say anything about my mother. She is the hardest working, sweetest, most beautiful person in the world. Second, she knows about being a lady because she is one. She's genteel, polite, nice, and helpful. She's the one who taught me that all girls are princesses."

"What makes you think all girls are princesses?"

"Because they are all noble and nice in their hearts!" Sarah said.

"Arguments based on *noblesse de cœur* do not count," Elwin said.

"What does that mean?" Lily asked.

"Yeah, it is rude to talk in other languages in front of people who can't understand them," Sarah said.

"It means nobleness of heart," he replied.

As they continued to walk and argue, Sarah and Lily became more and more angry. Once they crossed out of the pine trees and came to a road, Sarah thought seriously about leaving the mouse. He obviously was only tricking them the day before when he was being nice to them. He was not a mouse, he was a rat—mean, ugly, and selfish.

"Wait just a second," Elwin said. He stopped and looked around, then sighed a sigh of relief.

"What is it?" Sarah said, still a little angry.

"I want you to forgive the ugly things I have been saying for the last several minutes. You see, we just came through the whispering pines," Elwin explained.

"So?"

"So, they are supposed to be enchanted. Few people are able to pass through them. Many have just disappeared. I was not sure exactly why, but when we all started to feel sleepy, I guessed that the enchantment was one of sleep. We would have fallen asleep and never awakened. Didn't you feel sleepy?" Elwin asked.

"Yes," said Sarah. "Very sleepy."

"I wanted to take a nap," Lily said, which was not like her at all.

"Well, to keep us from falling asleep, I started an argument. I really did not mean anything I said. I was just being contrary."

"Oohh, I see," Sarah said. "You pretended to be mad at us to keep us from falling asleep. Why didn't you just tell us?"

"If you knew I was play acting, you may not have gone along, and you probably would not have gotten angry, which means you would have fallen asleep. It was the only way I could make sure we stayed awake," Elwin said.

"Why did you take us into the woods if they make you sleepy?" Sarah asked.

"I did not plan to. I was not exactly sure the location of the enchanted wood from the witch's cottage. I mean, I knew it was in this general direction, but I thought the path we were taking would lead us to the east of it. Unfortunately, I was a little off. After all, I have not traveled this way in a year or more, and I was much bigger then. As soon as we passed into the pines and I saw how quiet it was, I knew where we were. That is when I decided to start the argument."

"So have there been many other people disappear in the woods?" Lily asked.

"Yes. Some disappeared as long ago as when I was a child, some fifty years or more according to our time. There may have been some before then, but it was not well known at first. Of course, most people in the Kingdom of Fairie have heard about it by now, and those who know of it avoid it if they can, but sometimes people just wander into it as we did. I am a little surprised that we did not see anyone lying under the trees sleeping. Of course, they may be covered with pine needles or wild animals may have carried away their bones or something. You never know what is in the forest."

"Why would the forest be enchanted like that?" Sarah asked.

"It is probably a protection that some fairy or sprite put on it. If there are fairies living in the trees, what they call dryads, and the trees were destroyed, their homes would be gone. By protecting the forest from harmful people, they would be protecting themselves, and what better way to protect the forest than by having everyone that comes through fall asleep. Of course, that is just a guess. There is really no way of knowing for sure.

"So, are we all friends again?" Elwin added.

"Friends," said Sarah.

"Friends," said Lily.

Then they all shook hands and hugged.

"Now, are we all ready to continue on?" Elwin asked.

"Of course," said Sarah, "we may be little girls, but we can surprise you."

"You already have," said Elwin.

9

The Fairy Dragon

Once they were a long way from the whispering pines, Sarah, Lily, and the mouse Elwin stopped to rest overnight. Sarah and Lily pitched their tent between two roots of a tree. They got in their sleeping bags, but the mouse just curled up between them. Elwin said it was not safe to light a fire because it would attract all manner of creatures, including the servants of the witch, so they did without a hot supper, just some fruit and nuts, and cheese, of course. Fortunately, Elwin's fur helped keep them warm through the night, and the roots blocked the wind. The next morning, they risked a small fire to cook some breakfast and were careful to only use dry wood so that there would be very little smoke. They fried up some ham and eggs the fairies had given them, which was a very good way to start the day.

Sarah, Lily, and Elwin continued their march toward the lake, using the position of the sun to keep them moving in the right direction. They walked most of the morning without incident. Around noon, it started to rain, and they all pulled out their cloaks and raincoats and put on galoshes. Even Elwin had a cloak, which he had cut from the cloak of another elf the witch had captured. He also had little homemade boots, which he had made out of scrap pieces of rubber and some string. It was funny to see the mouse in the little boots, but he said he hated to get mud on his feet because it stuck to his fur. They stopped to eat a hot lunch to knock the chill off—some stew made of the ham with some potatoes that Elwin dug up heated over a fire—then they continued toward the lake again in the afternoon.

The rain quit after a while, and a fog settled in the forest. It gave all the trees an eerie look, with a pale light and tree shadows showing through the mist. It made traveling challenging, as it was difficult to know which direction the lake was. If it had not been for Elwin, they would have gotten lost quickly. He taught them that moss grew on the north side of certain types of trees. All they had to do was check the trees and keep moving in a northeasterly direction, and they would run into the lake.

At one point, the ground sloped sharply downward for several dozen yards. Afterwards, it seemed to level off.

"Ah," said Elwin, "This proves we are going the right way. Somewhere before the lake, there is a depression in the ground, basically a very wide pit or low area. It's about a quarter of a mile in diameter, but only thirty or forty yards deep, so it's easier to cut across it than go around it. From here, it is only about a mile or two to the lake. If we hurry, we should be able to make it by nightfall."

"If we can tell that it's night with all this fog," Sarah said.

"Be careful, though. The rain may have made it slick. And watch for puddles when we get to the bottom. Water usually collects in depressions."

The three plunged into the depression, grabbing hold of the trees on the way down to keep themselves from slipping. When they got to the bottom, there were indeed some very large puddles, along with some firm ground. Evidently, it had not rained enough to fill up the entire depression. Sarah, Lily, and Elwin started to make their way across the low ground. The mist was particularly thick at the bottom, almost like a sea of white, so they walked carefully, testing the ground in front of them with their walking sticks to stay on the high ground.

About midway across, the three came to a large field of mushrooms growing out of the mist. Still being mouse-sized, they found that most of the mushrooms were waist high or larger, and the field seemed to extend for a hundred yards or so, though it was probably only a few feet to big people. The mushrooms came in all sorts of shapes and sizes. Some of them were tall and skinny like towers. Others were short and fat with tops that spread around like a roof. Some were tiny, like an umbrella or stool. The three of them began to weave their way through the mushrooms, trying to keep their bearings by focusing on a particularly large oak tree on the far side as Elwin taught them. At some points, the three lost sight of the tree among the white and orange fungus growing around them, but they eventually broke into open sight of the tree and could correct their course.

When they were about halfway across, they stopped for a moment, and Lily looked up.

"What is that?" she wondered aloud.

Far above the mushroom patch was a small orb of pink light, like a bubble. At first, it was small and far away, but it gradually grew closer and larger until it hovered right above them getting as big as a hot air balloon. Gradually, the orb moved above a large, wide mushroom that was right in front of Sarah, Lily, and Elwin, and the orb slowly began to dissipate. The shadow of a figure within seemed to take shape before their eyes as the orb disappeared. They soon saw that it was a lizard of some kind. As the orb finally melted away, there sat before them a pink dragon, only with beautiful butterfly wings instead of the usual bat-like dragon wings. Flame curled from its lips, and smoke issued from its nostrils as it began to look around.

"It's a fairy dragon," Elwin whispered.

"What's a fairy dragon?" Sarah asked.

"They are small dragons, very magical and usually good, although often mischievous. Some say the fairy dragons were creations of elven magic, a cross between a fairy and a dragon, more fairy than dragon, really. That is why they are not very big. But don't let their size fool you. The fairy dragons have powerful magic and strong senses, they are usually very clever, and anyways, they are bigger than we are. Better let me talk to it. We elves have made a long study of dragons."

"Who is trespassing in my domain?" growled the dragon, their whispering apparently drawing its attention.

"Just three small travelers, not even worth the notice of a mighty serpent as yourself," said Elwin, who knew that the proper way to talk to a dragon was to praise it. This kind of talk seemed to please the beast, even though it was not on friendly terms. At least the thing is polite, thought Sarah.

"And what kind of travelers are they?" the dragon inquired, fire belching from its mouth with each inflection. "Two children who are a tenth of the size they should be and a mouse that talks. I smell something magical here."

"And wise you are, most magnificent and magical of dragon lords," Elwin responded. "For I have been enchanted by a witch, and these two children are under the protection of the Fairy Queen."

"Witch, eh? Fairy Queen? Well, this is my domain, not the Fairy Queen's. And there is no one to cure you from the witch's spell here."

The dragon spread its great wings, which were colored pink with purple swirls. As it moved the wings, the pattern seemed to move. Lily began to stare blankly at the wings and took a step forward. Elwin swept his cloak in front of Lily.

"Do not stare at its wings. They can entrance the unwary and make you the dragon's prey," he whispered to Sarah. She shielded her eyes, and Lily, now back to her senses, stepped behind her sister.

"Ha, ha, ha," laughed the serpent. "As though you can protect yourself from my magic."

Elwin replied, "We know indeed that it is no use to resist one so powerful. We had no desire to intrude on your lands. I have traveled through these lands often in the past and had no knowledge of a dragon in this part of the forest, although admittedly it has been nearly a year since last I traveled this road. I would have respectfully avoided your domains had I known. Certainly one so mighty can afford to allow small travelers to pass if they promise to never pass through these lands again."

"True it is that I am new to these lands, as I came here only a few months ago. Yet, if I allow some to pass, others will think that I am soft and open my lands to anyone. Then people will trespass day in and day out," the dragon said.

"We would certainly correct such a notion, perhaps by telling of our narrow escape and warning them of your mighty dominion over these lands."

"And what of the witch? If you are fleeing from her, as is apparent by what you have said—for everyone knows that the witch and Fairy Queen are enemies—what is to keep her from chasing you through here and venting her wrath upon me."

"But certainly, a witch is no match for such a powerful and wily dragon."

The serpent seemed to wince a little, as if reminded of something. Then it leaned forward, drumming its claws on the edge of the mushroom as it stared at them, considering. To Lily, the creature seemed a little sad.

"While I am almost persuaded by your logic," the dragon started a little reluctantly, "I am afraid that I must either enchant you, eat you, choke you with my tail, burn you to a crisp, or perhaps all of the above. I will let you decide the manner of your death, as I am feeling generous today."

"What do you think?" Elwin asked as they huddled together.

"I suppose I would prefer being enchanted by its magic. The other choices sound too gruesome to even contemplate," Sarah said.

"Not that," Elwin said. "Do not give up hope yet. I only meant, do you think we could outrun it? If I distract it through more conversation, you could start to back quietly away. When I say run, take off as fast as you can, using the mushrooms for cover. I will run a different direction. When you are away, make to the northeast. I will meet you on the shores of the lake."

Elwin stood up and faced the serpent. "You leave us with not much of a choice, as all lead to a horrible death. Could we not make some negotiation? Is there no service we could perform as penance for our misdeed, no way we could pay you for our passage?"

As he spoke, Sarah and Lily began to edge behind a mushroom.

"There is nothing that *I* can think of," the dragon said.

"What if we give you a gift? How about this nice elven cloak?" he said as he held up the cloak in front of its eyes. "Run," he whispered at the girls. They took off.

Suddenly, the cloak burst into flames as the dragon breathed on it. The dragon took off breathing fire as it flew through the ashes of the cloak hanging in the air. It circled around, setting the ground on fire directly behind the girls. They were trapped! Then it landed on another mushroom that guarded the side opposite to the fire. There was nowhere to run.

"Fool! Do you think I am so deaf that I cannot hear someone whispering a few feet away, let alone a hundred yards? Now, you leave me no choice."

It breathed in deeply as though it were going to set them all on fire. Then it looked at them closing their eyes in terror, but instead of breathing out, it slumped down, again looking kind of sad.

"Are we still alive?" Lily wondered.

"Why did it not destroy us?" Sarah asked.

"I think," answered Elwin, "It is because it is basically a good dragon, and it is not in its nature to destroy without cause. Is this not right, O mighty one?"

"Yes," the dragon said, a tear escaping from its eye only to sizzle and evaporate on its nose. "But you see, I must destroy you. The witch has a power over me that I cannot fight, and it is her will that you die."

"The witch knows we are here?" Sarah asked.

"No. At least, I do not know. She has ordered me to destroy all who come this way. Most I have been able to keep away using my magic, but for some reason, you were immune. It must be the protection of the fairies."

"How could you have fallen under the spell of the witch, you who are so powerful?" Elwin asked.

"It was not an enchantment. The witch has something of mine—an egg. She found my nest and stole my egg. She said that unless I did exactly what she said, she would turn it into an omelet. Do you have any idea how rare it is for my kind to mate and have children? I must do what I can to keep the egg from being destroyed because it may be my only offspring."

"But certainly you know that the witch will destroy it sooner or later, whether or not you do as she says," Elwin said. "Once your usefulness is gone and the witch can no longer control you, she will use the egg as a trap to destroy you or turn you into something harmless, as she did to me."

"I do not always think clearly where my child is concerned," the dragon said. "All I know is that if I did not obey, she would destroy the egg today, and I had to prevent that."

"What if we could get the egg back?" Sarah asked.

"Get my egg back? But how?"

"We are going now to find the fairy child. Then we are going to steal her wand. While we are there, we could find the egg and take it back to you," Sarah suggested.

"But I could not take a chance like that. If she were to find out, she would destroy the egg. Her second sight could reveal all," the dragon said.

"Ah, but she is not looking for us, and in fact has not seen us yet," Sarah said, "Even if she did learn of our existence, she would not know what we look like or where we are going. No, she could not find us that way."

"And with the struggle with the Fairy Queen, she is likely to be distracted. I doubt she is watching you so closely," said Elwin. "Besides, this might be the only chance you have to rescue your egg."

The dragon looked at them closely. She looked into Lily's and Sarah's eyes and knew she could trust them. Somehow, she knew that this was her one shot at getting the egg back, and that these children, so small but so determined, would be the ones to do it.

"Very well. I must take the chance. Go, but do not come back this way. No use in taking unnecessary risks of the witch knowing of our arrangement. When you find the egg, hold it in your hand and then summon me."

"How can we summon you?" Sarah asked.

"Just speak my name—T'srak L'agwenda—three times, and I will come to you, no matter where you are or how far away."

After the children repeated her name several times to learn it, they quickly departed as T'srak put out the fire and hid all signs of their passage. Then she disappeared again the same way that she had come—in a little pink bubble disappearing into the sky.

10

The Lake

Sarah, Lily, and Elwin left the dragon behind, climbed out of the depression, and continued the last mile through the woods to the lake. They arrived after dark. Since the light of the full moon lit up the land for miles around the lake, they decided to make camp for the night back among the trees some distance from the water to hide them from the witch's spies. The three went back from the lake about a dozen yards and found a large tree that was low to the ground and easy to climb. They figured that it would be safer up high if the servants of the witch patrolled the vicinity of the lake.

The particular tree the threesome chose had a low, wide limb they could almost walk onto from the trunk. It was more than wide enough to allow them to roll out their sleeping bags without their heads or feet hanging off. Lily was a little afraid without a railing because she rolled around a lot in bed, but she felt comfortable enough between Elwin and Sarah, who never moved while sleeping but stayed straight as a board.

The next morning, the girls and Elwin woke refreshed, but a little stiff from sleeping on the hard wooden limb. They found a sunny spot where they could eat breakfast and made a meal of some of the fairy bread and drink. Finally, after they had warmed and filled their stomachs, it was time to continue on this last stage of their mission.

The group marched down to the lake. It was quite beautiful with the trees just starting to change colors reflecting off the lake. In the morning sun, they could see the distant shore curving around to their right about a mile away. Interrupted only by the occasional bays or creeks pushing out into the forest, the shore roped around until it connected to the shore on which they stood. To their left, the lake seemed to go on for some distance. They could not see the end of it, only water, although they could see the far shore snaking in and out of inlets for some miles. Other than some reed beds near the shore, they could see only the flat sheet of water extending as far as the eye could see.

"So where is this Crow Island you talked about?" Sarah asked.

"That way, I believe," Elwin said. He pointed to the left down the lake. At first, they could see only water in that direction. When they strained, they could just make out where the water forked in two different directions at a peninsula, but there was no island in view.

"I can't see the island," Sarah said.

"You can see it from a little closer," Elwin said.

The girls and Elwin continued along the shore of the lake a little ways until they found an old fallen tree near the water. They climbed carefully through the roots to a branch poking up far above the water like a tower. From that vantage, they could see an island, which looked like a lifeless mound of earth in the middle of the left hand turn some hundred yards off shore.

The mouse pointed to the mound of earth. "There it is."

"That is far away, but even if we were closer, I don't think we could swim that far into the lake," Sarah said.

"Especially since I can't swim well," Lily added. She had only that summer learned to hold her breath, tread water, and do some basic strokes, but she was not good at them yet.

"We will have to figure out a way there, unless Elwin already has something planned," Sarah said.

"I did not say that I had a way to get on the island; I just said I knew where it was," Elwin replied. "Perhaps, if we walk around the lake, we could find a boat or something.

There are a lot of settlements on the lake, so we are bound to run into something sooner or later. Of course, we would not be able to operate it as small as we are, but perhaps we can get some big people to operate it or steal a ride."

"Yes," Sarah said, "Or perhaps we could use the potion to make us big once we get to that point. I know how to operate a boat, or at least a canoe. Daddy used to take us out on the river at the camp grounds. I've seen him use the oar many times."

Everyone had forgotten about the potion, but it made perfect sense once they found a boat. So the three of them started to walk around the edge of the lake in the direction of the island. It would not hurt to work their way a little closer, even if they did not find a boat. It would mean less paddling, and Sarah and Lily knew how hard it was to paddle after seeing their father and mother row a long way.

Elwin and the girls walked at a brisk pace knowing that they had almost completed the task before them. But that did not keep them from enjoying the day. The sun was shining, the trees were just starting to change colors, and the sun reflected off the lake, which was like a beautiful mirror. The lake was really a deep, slow part of the river, if they had known, cut off from the rest of the river with dams. The particular part of the lake near the island, however, was very rocky, and the island itself was relatively flat and treeless, so few people ever went there. In fact, the only creatures they saw near the island were the crows after which the island was named. They would fly back and forth from their nest at the top of the mound on the island.

"I would suggest trying to catch a ride with the crows," Elwin said, "But crows are such dirty and generally selfish creatures. I doubt they would do anything to help you, even if we could communicate with them."

After a few hours of walking, they started to draw near the island, but still they had run across neither dwellings nor a boat of any kind. It was, of course, slow going because of their size. Finally, about noon, they stopped to eat some nuts and berries and drank water. After this quick bite, the three returned to their march, hoping that they would find a boat before it was too late in the day, when they would be forced to spend another night in the witch's territory.

About the middle of the afternoon, Sarah, Lily, and Elwin approached what looked like a small hut on the side of the lake across a road that led down to the water's edge. The hut was only a foot or so high, perfect size for a fairy or leprechaun. But knowing that this was the witch's domain, they waited in some grass across the road to make sure it was not one of the dark elves or some other servant of the witch. After a few minutes, their fears were confirmed. A little man walked to the front of the hut and sat down on the grass.

Even Sarah knew that this was not an elf or fairy, but a brownie. Most brownies lived in old houses, but there were also forest brownies, which were a little more primitive, like this one. He was no more than six or seven inches tall, with clothes made of woven grass fiber, a spear, and a helmet made of what looked like a hollowed out bird's skull, with the beak pointing out over his head like the bill on a baseball cap.

"We're in luck," said Elwin. "If it were a dark elf, we would be up against strong magic, and goblins are tough and just plain mean. But brownies, although they can be tricky and mischievous, are usually not very focused on assigned tasks. Perhaps we can distract it or outwit it if we stay alert. Follow my lead."

"Hello, old man," Elwin said approaching the brownie. The girls followed Elwin across the road until they stood in front of the hut.

"I'm not a man. I'm a brownie," he said gruffly without getting up and without looking at them.

"That I can see."

"And you're not a man, you're a mouse. If you're looking for cheese, you've come to the wrong place."

"No, no cheese, thank you. Any more than you would like a cat," Elwin said.

The brownie look startled and finally got up.

"And what would a mouse and two little girls be doing wandering around in the woods. And a talking mouse at that."

"Actually," said Elwin, "We were looking for a boat to get to the other side. Do you happen to know where one is?"

"Certainly," the brownie said. He walked to the edge of the water and pulled up an old brown leaf resting against a tree stump. "For a price, you can use my boat."

"That's a boat?" asked Sarah. "It looks like a leaf."

"Of course it is a boat. It's a magical leaf. Give it a try."

Elwin sat in the leaf carefully, and the girls pushed him off the shore. The leaf coasted out a foot from the edge, then quickly sank, leaving Elwin sitting in water up to his chin.

"Haw, haw, haw," the brownie laughed. "If you want, I can shake this tree and get you a yacht with a bedroom."

Elwin climbed out of the water and shook his fur, spraying water and mud all over the brownie, who then proceeded to wipe off his face with its hands. Angry at being fooled, Elwin charged the brownie, but the brownie disappeared at the last moment into thin air. Elwin looked around and, knowing that the old man had disappeared and that he would never catch the brownie, came back to his senses. He wondered if he could make the brownie appear. Then he got another idea.

"Ah, I should have known it," Elwin said to the girls. "This brownie has no boat and cannot get across the water. Not only is he dishonest, he is land-locked like all his people."

"I did not say that I couldn't get across the water," said the brownie, reappearing a few feet away.

"How could you without a boat?" Elwin asked.

"I have my ways."

"After what you just showed us, I have my doubts."

"Oh, really! Well, it just so happens that I don't need a boat because I can fly."

"Brownies can't fly; everyone knows that. They don't have wings."

"With help I can," the brownie said.

"And who would help a brownie?" Elwin asked.

"A dragonfly. They come when I call."

"This is the first I've heard of a domesticated dragonfly. I think you are only fooling me again. No, we will be on our way," Elwin said.

"I can prove it," the brownie bragged. He turned around and whistled a shrill whistle three times. A dragonfly flew to the edge of the lake, and the brownie carefully stepped onto it. The dragonfly then took off into the air. The brownie circled around over the surface of the lake and returned to the same spot, climbing carefully off.

"Let me try," said Elwin.

"You are way too big to ride. Besides, they only answer to my call."

"Then what use is it to me?" Elwin asked.

"I did not say it was useful to *you*. You asked only why I did not need a boat. Haw, haw, haw. There are no boats here, no way of crossing the water, unless you want to hike another five or ten miles to the west to the nearest human settlements. Now, get lost."

The three of them walked past the hut and continued down the lake until the hut and brownie were out of sight and sound.

"What a rude fellow!" Sarah said.

"What are we going to do now?" Lily asked.

"Don't worry your pretty little head," Elwin said. "The fool gave away all we need to know. You heard the brownie whistle, didn't you?"

"Yes," Sarah and Lily said at the same time.

"Well, all you have to do is whistle in the exact same pitch and length. He worked no magic to make the thing come. I would have seen it. It should come for anyone who calls. All you have to do is whistle."

Sarah and Lily looked at him.

"Can't you whistle?"

They shook their heads.

"Really? You should probably learn. It can come in very handy, and then you can make your own music. Very well, I suppose I can do it, although it is a little difficult for me with this mouse's snout," he said.

He walked to the edge of the lake and blew, but it did not come out as a whistle. He put his hand to his mouth and whistled, only it came out the wrong pitch and was too short. He tried again and got the length of the notes right, but was still too sharp in the pitch. Finally, after another two or three more tries, Elwin hit the notes exactly. Immediately, a dragonfly appeared on the edge of the water. He whistled two more times in the same manner, and two more dragonflies appeared. They were strange-looking creatures with large, bulbous, multi-faceted and otherworldly eyes and a long, narrow, cigar-shaped body of fluorescent green. Elwin tried to get on one, but the thing had to beat its wings fiercely and even then it could not keep from dipping slightly into the water.

"Drat! The dirty little brownie is right. I am too big," Elwin said.

"Maybe you could balance on two of them," Sarah suggested.

"That would be too difficult. Best not to try it. No matter. The island is right across the lake, and there is plenty of daylight left for you to finish your task. You will have to go across on your own."

"But we could never go without you," Sarah said. "Besides, those bugs look creepy, and I hate insects."

"It will be all right," Elwin said. "I can wait around here. That way, I can hear you if you call or see you if you signal. If necessary, I can get some limbs and make a raft, though it might take a little time. As for the dragonflies, they are quite harmless. They eat only flies and mosquitoes, nothing as big as us. And these are really quite tame."

"I don't know," Sarah said.

"Well, it's either ride the dragonflies now and get it over with, walk another few days down the lake, or spend tomorrow and possibly the next day cutting off limbs and gathering vines to make a raft. And you know, after we talked to the brownie, he could tip off the witch at any moment, which really leaves us with very little time."

"I guess when you put it that way," Sarah replied.

Sarah turned to the dragonflies, and Lily was already climbing on the smallest of the three. Elwin helped Sarah get on another one. Her face wrinkled up as she touched it.

"Its skin feels yucky," Sarah said.

"Put your cloak down to sit on and use it to hold on," Elwin suggested.

Sarah obeyed and was able to get on, straddling a leg on either side of its head. She heard a slight buzzing as the wings beat quickly. The wings were almost invisible, they moved so quickly. Yet the dragonfly remained perfectly still. Elwin then shooed off the third.

"Just head straight toward the lake," Elwin said.

"How do we make it go?" Sarah asked.

"I think the brownie used his knees," Elwin replied.

Sarah pushed both her knees in slightly, and the thing took off like a bullet. It took her a few seconds to get her bearing. The dragonfly was moving so fast that the wind was creating suction against her face, forcing her eyes closed. Finally, she forced one eye open. The lake was going by quickly, and she was heading away from the island down the lake. She tried pulling on its back and pushing with her hands, but it kept on straight. Then she remembered about the knees, and dug in her left knee into its shoulder. The dragonfly turned right. She tried the other leg, and it turned left. After only a few minutes, she could control it perfectly.

Only then did Sarah remember Lily. She looked around the lake. Lily was already far from the vicinity of the island, so Sarah turned around and headed back, looking for Lily. At last, she saw Lily on the other dragonfly heading across the water toward the far shore. Sarah dug in both knees and the dragonfly sped up until she was right beside Lily.

"Use your knees," Sarah shouted. "Push in your knees to make it go faster. Use the knee on this side to make it go that way, and that side to make it go this way."

Lily nodded. Soon she had turned her dragonfly around, and they were cruising side by side over the water. It was by far the most exhilarating ride they ever had. It was much better than a roller coaster or boat. It reminded Sarah a little of riding on a jet ski with her mother one time at the lake when she was young, only the dragonfly could turn without any effort and was much faster because it never touched the water. They whizzed all over the lake, practicing turning sharply and gently.

"We had better go to the island," Sarah said. Lily agreed.

The girls turned the dragonflies and headed straight toward the shore of the island, which was coming on fast. Sarah suddenly realized that they did not know how to stop the dragonflies. She tried pushing in her knees, but it only went faster. She tried rubbing them, and combining using her knees with her hands. Nothing seemed to slow it down. They were about to fly right over the island when Lily figured it out.

"Use your knee and your heel," Lily said.

Sarah pushed in her knee while pulling her heel up to its underside. Dragonflies can stop on a dime if they want, and in this case, the dragonfly stopped almost immediately just as they came up to the shore. Although the dragonfly stopped, Sarah kept on going, throwing her off the dragonfly's back and onto the ground. She rolled head over heels to a stop some feet later. She looked around, and Lily was right beside her rubbing her head.

"I'm OK," Lily said.

"My, they stop suddenly," Sarah said as she stood up and dusted herself off. "Maybe next time we should learn to stop before we take off."

"That would be a good idea," said Lily.

Sarah walked over to her winged steed and got her and Lily's cloaks from the back of the dragonflies.

"Thank you for the ride," Sarah said, and both of their steeds flew away. She helped Lily get up, and they stood looking at the island. They finally had made it.

11

Crow Island

Sarah and Lily stood for a moment looking at the island before them. It was not very large, certainly no more than a hundred yards across and fifty or so wide, though at their size it seemed quite a bit larger. There were no plants or trees—only small river stones and rocks and an occasional piece of driftwood. The island was mostly flat except for a large mound at one end towering several dozen feet high like a mountain before them. They could see black birds from which the island got its name circling around the top of the mound, with their caws echoing eerily across the lake. On the other end of the island, barely visible in the rock, were the square remains of the foundation of a building, only a few inches of which were not buried in rock and clay. It was, then, more than just a temporary or recently formed island, as was common in the river. It had been someone's home.

"Well, we are here," Sarah said. "Now, all we need to do is find the fairy child, if he is here at all. But where do we look, and what does he look like?"

"If he's turned to stone, the fairy child will look like a rock," Lily said.

The girls looked around at all the rocks on the shore. There were thousands of them. Maybe even millions.

"It's like looking for a needle in a haystack," said Sarah. "We will never find the child among all of these rocks."

"But the fairy child would not look like all of these rocks," Lily reasoned slowly. "He would be a rock that looked like a child, wouldn't he? With arms and legs and wings. And since the child is special, the rock probably would be, too."

It was so simple that Sarah saw that it had to be right. "You mean, maybe it's shiny or made of gold or something?"

"That's it! It's shiny or something," Lily responded.

The girls spread out and started looking around the island, turning over rocks and logs and moving the ones they could lift out of the way to look under them. They made their way slowly forward to make sure they did not overlook anything. A few times, they thought they found something that might be it. One time Lily found a golden, shiny-looking rock, but Sarah told her it was fool's gold. Besides, it was a square chunk, not fairy child-shaped. A little later, Sarah found a rock that looked like a person rolled up into a ball, sort of. But it was rough around the edges and not an exact statue-like figure of a person, as you would expect with someone turned to stone. Anyway, it was too big to be a child if it was really someone turned to stone, and it was not shiny or special.

Sarah and Lily made their way along the island until they reached the foot of the mound. Since there were no rocks on the mound, they continued along the shore around it until they reached the far end. Not having found anything, they turned around and started making their way toward the end of the island from which they came.

"Perhaps it is not lying on the beach," Sarah said, stopping to rest a moment. "Perhaps the witch put it into a hole or a buried box for safe-keeping. Otherwise, it might get lost or wash away. If that's the case, we could look for days and not find it unless we have some clues."

"Maybe if there was a box, it would be buried where the house was," Lily said.

The girls went to where the remains of the foundation were. The foundation was a square outline of the building made of bricks that just barely stuck out above ground level. It was only about ten or twenty feet from end to end with three rooms—one larger room and a smaller room on each end, which they guessed were a living area and the bathroom and kitchen. They figured that a small house had stood there many years before. Perhaps the witch herself lived there, but at the very least it was one of her servants who she had left there to guard the island. This would suggest that it was one time a very important place, maybe a prison or treasury.

It would make sense for the witch to bury a box with important things on a distant island far from her home, so they started searching the ground. Sarah and Lily poked around the dirt and stones in the center of the house looking for the remains of a staircase. They then did the same around the outer edge of the house looking for a cellar door, but there was nothing there. They even checked to see if there was an echo under the ground where a cellar might have been, but the earth seemed solid. They walked around the foundation looking for a cubby hole among the stones, but there did not appear to be any holes in the rocks. Finally, they wandered about for forty or fifty feet looking for an area where the earth was recently overturned. They spent over an hour searching carefully, but they found nothing at all.

"Well, let's give the island one last look before we give up for the day," Sarah said.

They started to make their way across the island again, looking here and there among the rocks. As they approached the mound, Sarah looked up toward its peak and saw the crows circling overhead. One seemed to be circling ever lower. In fact, it seemed to be diving toward them. The crow streaked down straight toward them!

"Run!" Sarah said. Lily took off like a marathon runner followed by Sarah.

The crow swooped narrowly overhead, its claws hanging down menacingly. Sarah and Lily dove and lay flat on the ground as the crow whizzed past them. They looked up and saw it turning around and climbing for another dive. Sarah looked around and saw a piece of driftwood with several branches sticking down into the sand like bars on a cage.

"Follow me," she said, getting up and running toward the driftwood. Lily got up and followed.

By then, the crow had turned around and was ready for another run. It dove at them, but Sarah and Lily ran behind the driftwood, and the crow pulled up. Soon they saw another crow join the first and start to dive. Sarah and Lily backed up as far as they could go under the driftwood. One of the crows dove and pulled up again. The other landed near them. Sarah instinctively grabbed a small twig and started poking at the bird as it tried to reach around the branches of the driftwood.

"What does it want?" Sarah screamed. "I thought crows ate corn."

"Maybe it wants that," Lily said, pointing to Sarah's necklace, which was sparkling in the sun, reflecting into the crow's eyes.

It was a silver necklace shaped like an "S", which Sarah always wore. But she had not noticed it sparkling before. She immediately took it off and put it into her pocket. The crow continued to peck at them for a few minutes, but it soon lost interest and flew off to join its mate in the skies.

After they were sure the crows would not return, they rested a few minutes. Sarah said, "That gives me an idea."

"What?" asked Lily.

"If crows like shiny things and the fairy child is shiny, wouldn't they have picked him up and carried him back to their nest?"

Lily looked up the mound. "You mean we have to go up there?"

"It might be the only way to get the child."

"How can we get up there without the crows noticing us?" Lily wondered.

"First of all, we don't wear anything shiny. They don't seem to pay attention to us much if it's just us. Then we put on the elven cloaks so that we blend into the dirt. Once we get up there, we move quickly into and out of the nest without drawing a lot of attention to ourselves. We only need to scope the place out and see if the fairy child is there. If he's not, we will leave quietly without disturbing anything."

Finally, Lily agreed, knowing that this was the only way to complete their mission. So, the girls carefully removed anything shiny—Lily took off some sparkly scrunchies that were in her hair, and Sarah changed shirts because her shirt had some gold thread in it. Then they put on the elven cloaks, and Lily was careful to cover all of her shiny blond hair. With that done, they started the slow climb up the mound.

Sarah and Lily walked carefully, looking for the easiest path. There was no road, per se, but there were long flat places across the tops of dirt clods or where the ground leveled out momentarily. By zigzagging back and forth, the girls were able to stay on the paths. All the while, the crows flew back and forth overhead not paying them any attention. It was not until they were near the top that the climb turned difficult. First, there was a steep incline without ledges or flat spots. Then there was what looked like part of an old tree rising above that. Because of the way the mound sloped, they had not really noticed it from the ground. The top of the tree was gone. All that was left was a stump with several large holes on one side, which is where the crows kept their nests.

Once Sarah and Lily reached the highest spot they could climb, Sarah sat down to think about how to continue. She remembered Daddy's rope and made a slipknot in it like Daddy had shown her. She edged around to the side of the stump opposite of the holes from which the crows emerged. Then she threw her lasso and missed hitting anything. She tried again and again with no success. Perhaps if she threw it with more of a side-armed lob, she thought, she might get it higher. She tried this, but it went past the limb for which she was aiming. She tried reeling it back in, but it was caught on something. She pulled hard, but it was stuck fast. Now was the time. She waited until there were no crows in sight, and then started to climb up, half walking on the cliff or tree, half pulling with her arms.

When she made it to the top, she tried pulling the rope loose, but she was unable. Instead, she threw the end of the rope down to Lily.

"Tie it around your waist and yank on it when you are done," Sarah yelled to Lily.

Lily started to work on something. After a few minutes of fiddling with the rope, Lily yanked. Sarah started to pull her up. Lily was very heavy, and several times Sarah let the rope slip. Finally, Sarah started to use her head. She pulled the rope up, then threw a loop around a branch coming off the stump. Then she returned, grabbed another length of rope, pulled it up, and tied it off. It was hard work, but in a few minutes, Lily was at the top. Sarah was amazed that Lily had made it at all. The knot she put in the rope looked like a rat's nest with rope going here and there and everywhere.

The girls left the rope for their escape, waited for a time when no crows were close by, and then inched around the edge of the cliff to the holes in the stump. Quickly, they slid inside.

It was really a community nest. There was a large chamber in the middle where the center of the stump had rotted. There were chambers around the edge where each mother made her nest. The girls quickly moved over to one of the holes that was unoccupied to get out of the center chamber, for birds seemed to be constantly coming in and out. Inside the first chamber was a nest made of grass and a lot of other things—string, ribbon, bottle caps, money, and a ring. But there was no fairy child. They waited until the center chamber was empty, and then they tiptoed into the next chamber. Inside they found another nest, with some shredded magazines, a piece of shiny Christmas wrapping paper, some tinsel, more money, and a necklace pendant, without the chain. The next chamber was occupied, so they did not go in it but moved to the one after that.

The fourth chamber contained more ribbon, a shiny potato chip bag (empty), a brass shotgun shell casing, and some shiny rocks. Immediately, the girls began to go through these. They found another piece of fool's gold, a cut piece of amethyst, and some assorted pebbles of different sizes and shapes. Finally, they found a beautiful piece of white crystal about the size of a field pea, which was just about baby-size if you were a fairy. Sarah picked it up in her arms and turned it around. It was shaped like a small child in the fetal position. They could easily make out details in the stone such as hands, bedclothes, pajamas, a hat, and even folded wings.

"This is it!" Sarah said. She took the stone, and put it into her bag, carrying the stone like a little papoose. "Now all we have to do is climb down and call the dragonflies."

Just then it occurred to them, as it probably has to you, that since neither of them could whistle, they could not call the dragonflies to return. In short, they were stuck on the island.

"How are we going to get the dragonflies to return?" Lily asked.

"I don't know. Perhaps we can get Elwin's attention and get him to call them. Or maybe we will have to wait on him to make a raft. He'll know what to do. Come on, let's go back to the shore. We can signal him from there."

Sarah and Lily started to make their way out of the nest, when they heard a crow approaching the outside of the hole. Quickly, they ducked down behind the empty potato chip bag and other trash. The crow entered, dropped something behind the nest, and then turned around and sat down with its head only inches from the hole. Sarah and Lily waited patiently, hoping that it would leave, but it just sat there picking at its feathers with its beak or cawing at the other birds flying in and out of the nest. The crow was too close to the hole for them to squeeze out, at least not without it noticing them. They looked around for another way out, but there wasn't one. Sarah and Lily were trapped!

12

Escape

Sarah and Lily waited inside the crow's nest for what seemed an hour for the crow blocking the exit to leave. Every now and then, it would stand up or look out the hole only to sit down again. They could hear crows coming in and out of the nest. Soon it would be dark. They were afraid what might happen if they were trapped in the nest overnight. At any moment, the crows might bump into them, mistake them for a morsel of food, and tear them apart with their razor-sharp bills. And think of how it would worry Elwin, who was waiting on the shore of the lake for them to return or give word.

"We're never going to get out of here," Sarah whispered in Lily's ear.

"Maybe when they go to sleep, we can sneak out," Lily whispered back.

"I don't think we can chance it. There's not much room between the bird and the door. Besides, I don't want to stay any longer than I have to."

Lily nodded in agreement.

The girls had to get out, and soon. All they really needed was a plan. The only way to get out was for the crow to leave. The only way the crow might leave was if it left to look for food or was frightened somehow. But even if they could get out of the hole, it did not solve the problem of getting off the island. Since they could not summon the dragonflies that carried them to the island, they would have to find some other way. They might get Elwin to make a raft, but that could take days. No, there had to be another way.

Sarah looked around.

"There's a lot of stuff in these crows' nests. Perhaps we could use some of this stuff to help us escape," she whispered. Lily nodded.

Sarah and Lily both looked around. The idea of using the potato chip bag as a boat or sail or something came to mind. Or perhaps they could fold the Christmas paper they saw in another hole into a boat. Sarah had actually seen someone fold paper to make a hat that looked like a boat. Origami, she thought it was called. Or perhaps they could build a raft using some of the items that float as buoys, like an empty shotgun shell. If they could plug the end, it would float, and they could build a raft on top of it and other hollow items. Of course, that would require them to get the stuff out of the nest, which would be difficult with the crows flying around them. In any case, they could go ahead and get some things in case they needed them. Since they lost their rope, some ribbon would be a good start. Sarah grabbed some ribbon and quietly rolled it up and put it into her bag.

The crow got up again and strutted around the nest, only this time, it did not sit back down. Instead, it stuck its head out the hole as if getting ready to leave. If it was leaving, they could try to sneak out to the shore of the island. If only they could just fly off like the crow, it would be a lot less work. Suddenly, Sarah had an idea.

"Quick, Lily, go stand next to the crow's feet."

Lily did as she was told, and Sarah stood next to her and pulled out the ribbon. Then she quickly started wrapping the ribbon around them both and then around the crow's leg. She wrapped again and again and again. Soon, they were both tied fast to the crow's foot.

As it turned out, Sarah's guess was correct. The crow stepped out of the nest and walked toward the entrance. In a few seconds, Sarah and Lily were flying underneath the crow across the lake. The crow noticed that they were there and tried at first to shake them loose, but Sarah had tied the ribbon tightly. It could not grab at them in mid-flight, so it continued on its way toward the shore. It looked like they were heading more or less in the right direction. But then the crow continued past the shore. Farther and farther inland, it seemed to fly.

"Wait," Sarah shouted, "Put us down! We want off near the lake! Where are you going? Elwin will sit there waiting on us."

"Good-bye, Elwin," Lily shouted.

After a few minutes, the lake was out of sight, and the crow started to head down toward a field. It got lower and lower and started to head right toward a fence surrounding a garden. In fact, they were flying straight at a fence post, and the crow did not seem to be slowing down. Instead, it lowered its legs like it was trying to knock them loose.

"Oh, no!" Sarah cried. They were going to be smashed against the fence. She started to fumble with the knot on the ribbon, hoping to get loose before it was too late. Lily closed her eyes.

Right at the last moment, the crow pulled up, and they missed the fence. Instead, it landed on a man's shoulder. Sarah finished untying the ribbon. It was none too soon! Immediately on landing, the crow started to peck at its feet to get the ribbon off (and whatever else was weighing it down). Luckily, Sarah and Lily were already free. The girls slid down into the man's shirt pocket.

Looking up out of the pocket, Sarah and Lily saw the crow fly away. They were off the island. The only problem was they were trapped again, and this time, they did not know where they were. If the man found them, he would no doubt kill them thinking they were mice, or worse, he might be a servant of the witch and turn them over to her. They sat in silence waiting for the man to grab at them, but he never did. Obviously, he did not see or feel them slip into his pocket. They waited a little longer, wondering if he was going to take them somewhere. Perhaps he would walk near the lake, and they could jump into the water. But the man did not move. In fact, he did not move at all. His head remained in the same place. They could not feel his arms or legs or anything else move. It was as if he were turned to stone or stuffed like a bird.

Stuffed! Sarah pushed against the man's breast. She heard the distinct sound of straw. It was not a man. It was a scarecrow. She climbed out of the pocket and onto the scarecrow's shoulder. Sure enough, she could see that under his hat the scarecrow had a burlap bag as a head with his face painted on it. She looked down and saw a pole coming out of his pant's leg, holding him off the ground. They almost laughed.

"Well, how do we get down?" Lily asked.

"Climb, I guess."

Sarah started to climb down the man's shirt using the buttons as a ladder. Lily followed, but lost her footing and slipped. As she fell past the edge of the coat, she grabbed onto a string hanging loose. It started to pull out with her. However, it slowed her down, so that by the time the string had pulled loose, Lily was right above the ground. Lily let go and dropped down on her feet. Sarah continued to climb down, eventually sliding down the scarecrow's pants and landing in the rolled up pants cuff near the ankle. From there Sarah vaulted onto the ground.

"Show off!" she said to Lily, smiling.

"Which way to the lake?" Lily asked.

"I can't even see out of the garden," Sarah responded. They stood looking a moment as the sun started to set, casting long shadows over the plants around them. Sarah started to look through her things and found the potion. Now was the time they needed to be big.

"Of course," Sarah said. She pulled out the bottle and unstopped it. It bubbled some green liquid, and it smelled perfectly horrible. "Do you want to try it, first?"

Lily put her hand over her mouth and shook her head.

"OK. I guess I should do it. But take the bottle from me quickly. If I should shoot up like Alice in Wonderland, you need to be able to reach the potion. Now, just one mouthful."

"No need to worry about that," Lily said, obviously disgusted by the liquid.

Sarah took only a mouthful as the Fairy Queen had taught them. Sarah quickly handed the bottle to Lily. At first, nothing happened. She started to say that it did not work, but then she noticed that Lily was getting smaller, as were the giant plants. It was not as fast as Alice in Wonderland, certainly not like a telescope unfolding. It was much more gradual, like riding an elevator in a tall building until, without notice, you are on the top floor looking down. And what a view it was! It looked like she could see for miles and miles. Perhaps she drank too much. She looked at the scarecrow, and she was about the right height, up to its waist. Her feeling of being too tall must have been that she had become so used to being so small.

Once Sarah was big, she waited for several minutes, wondering whether Lily had dropped the potion or simply did not want to take it. Quite suddenly, Lily seemed to appear next to her from nowhere. It was the magic, of course, that made it seem so sudden from the outside yet so gradual from the inside. Lily looked around. She seemed just the right size, too. Lily handed the potion to Sarah, who put it in her pack as she shuffled her things around. The fairy child, which she had set to the side next to the scarecrow so it would remain the right size, she now put into safekeeping in the chest pocket of her jacket and safely buttoned it.

"Now, let's go find Elwin," Sarah said, once she had everything settled.

Sarah and Lily looked around and saw some trees on the other side of the fence. They walked along the fence to a gate, and then they made for the trees. Once they were in the forest again, they started to check for moss on the trees as Elwin had taught them. Once they knew the direction, they headed northeast again, hoping that the lake was still in the same general direction.

A few minutes later, they arrived at the shore of the lake. The girls looked up and down the lake and saw far to their right Crow Island. They had arrived much farther to the west than the island and so had to backtrack, but the walk took a lot less time since they were big. After a few minutes' walk, they made it to the part of shore where they had left Elwin waiting for them. Of course, they could not find the exact spot; everything seemed so different from their higher point of view. But they knew they were close.

Sarah and Lily waited for several minutes, but did not see Elwin. They called for him, but no one answered. He wouldn't have left them, but could he have gotten captured? They were not sure. Or maybe he did not recognize them at their height and was frightened by them.

"Should we leave him?" Lily asked. "If he got captured, the bad people might be waiting for us, too."

"I'm worried, too. But Elwin was the one who knew the way back. And we know that if he can make it, he will meet us here. It's getting dark. Perhaps we should stay the night in this general area. If he does not find us by morning, we can try to find our way back."

Lily agreed, so they found a spot a little ways from the lake where they could make camp. Since they were alone, they decided to take a chance with a fire. It was not just that they were hungry, although they were; they thought the light might help Elwin find them in the dark. They pitched their tent, and Sarah made the fire just like she saw Daddy do it when they went camping. Soon, they were heating some ham and potatoes—what they had left from the previous day's meal—in a pan over the fire. After a hot meal, which they greatly enjoyed, they got into their tent. It was the first time that they had camped out in the woods by themselves, and they were sort of scared of the dark night. Every time an owl hooted or a frog croaked, they jumped up and looked around. They did not remember all of these sounds when they camped in the barn or even when they went camping with their family. Perhaps, Sarah thought, they were worried about Elwin and were straining their ears for any sound, or maybe they had simply been too tired and fell asleep too quickly. Eventually, after sitting, listening to the noises for a while, they huddled together in the tent and tried to forget everything and get some sleep.

A few minutes later, the girls heard some twigs snapping. Sarah opened an eye and looked out toward the fire, but she saw nothing suspicious. A little bit later, she heard their frying pan, which was lying on a rock next to the fire, fall onto the ground. This time, she raised her head, but she did not see anything near the pan. It must have been the wind blowing it over. Next, she heard a scraping noise, like something rubbing against the pan. This time, she got up and walked over to the pan, afraid she would find a ghost or snake or something.

There in the pan stood Elwin! He was scraping up some of the food left in the pan. No wonder she saw nothing when she looked.

"Elwin! We were so worried about you. What are you doing?" Sarah asked.

"Getting something to eat. I was out on the lake in a raft trying to get to the island when I heard you call. You must have gotten off the island without my seeing it. I tried calling back, but I guess you could not hear me because of my size. So I rowed back. Unfortunately, because of the current, I landed a little downstream. By the time I got back, you had already gone to sleep, so I figured I would get myself something to eat without waking you."

Lily heard him squeaking and got out of bed. Seeing him, she picked him up and hugged him, nearly squeezing the life out of him. They quickly told him what had happened, and they all lay down to sleep, happy to be together again.

13

Not Home

The next morning, Sarah, Lily, and Elwin woke up early, ate a hasty breakfast, and started the long march back to the witch's cottage. It had taken them two days and three nights to get to the island when they were tiny. Since the girls were now their normal size, they estimated it should not take more than a day to get back, provided they did not stop or run into any of the witch's servants.

"You can ride sitting on my shoulder," Sarah said to Elwin. "And if you get tired, you can sit in my shirt pocket."

"But I want him to ride on my shoulder," Lily said.

"I know you do, Lily, but I need him to sit up as high as possible so he can help tell us which way to go. Otherwise, we might get lost or run into trouble."

"However," Elwin said, "If I get tired, I will rest in your pocket, Lily."

The three agreed and left at once. Rather than backtrack and go through the fairy dragon's lair again, they cut directly to the southwest from where they were, which was perhaps two hours' walk to the west of where they needed to be. Elwin said they could correct their course after they crossed an old road.

"Once we get to the witch's cottage, we can cross the bridge and summon the fairies the way that they told us," Sarah said.

"Perhaps we should get the wand, first," said Elwin. "It will do the fairies no good to have the fairy child without the wand. And you know I want to be free from this animal nature. Besides, I know exactly where she keeps the wand, so it should be no problem finding it, provided that she left the wand there when she went out, as she often does, or that we can distract her if she is home."

That is what Sarah, Lily, and Elwin were all worried about—the witch being at home. Sarah and Lily had only seen her asleep and did not know exactly what to expect, but Elwin had told them of how wicked she was, and how she fed fairies to the cat or kept them in cages. Obviously, she was powerful. She had turned Elwin into a mouse and fairies into stone. In fact, the girls and Elwin were counting on her not being home. It was the only way they could get the wand and fulfill their mission. All of their thoughts now turned to their final destination.

The day went swiftly by, and they made pretty good time. In only an hour or so, the lake was far away. The day warmed up nicely, but with a crisp autumn breeze that blew every so often to keep them from working up a sweat. By lunchtime, they had come to the road that Elwin had mentioned.

"Funny that we did not see this road before," Lily said.

"Not really," said Elwin. "It does not cross between the cottage and the lake; it runs more parallel to the path we took, well at an angle, really."

"It would have been useful had we known about it," Sarah said.

"We could not afford to be seen," Elwin responded. "In addition to her second sight, the witch has many spies, and they would have spotted us easily if we had just walked down the middle of the road."

"Really? You mean she might have had us watched all along? I never thought of that," Sarah said, casting a doubtful glance around her. "What about now? How are we going to get across without being seen?"

"First thing we need to do is wait until later in the day, when shadows fall across the road. Then we find a place that is particularly dark and cross there. We can also try camouflaging ourselves, maybe with some branches or perhaps I can hide under a tin can or something. Anyway, let's get off the road to where we can't be seen and stop to eat, then we can move up the road after lunch."

They retreated into a shady spot in the woods and laid out a picnic lunch—ham slices on crackers, nuts, fruit, and water. Luckily, Sarah had been carrying the food on her when she became big, or there would not have been enough to go around. After lunch, they rested for a few minutes, lounging on their cloaks on the grass. Then they took off through the woods along the edge of the road.

The problem was that the three friends had to follow the road without actually traveling on it during the brightest time of day when anyone watching would be able to see them. So they walked through the woods, always keeping within sight of the road, yet always staying under cover. They made pretty good time until they came to a steep hill. The road cut straight through it, leaving a steep cliff facing the road. Because of how the rocks were piled up, they could not climb it. At least the girls could not climb it. Being a mouse, Elwin could have made it, but it would have taken even him a long time.

"What do we do now?" asked Sarah. "If we stay by the road, we will have to walk out into the open."

"Yes, and unfortunately, the road turns sharply to the right just above this pass," Elwin said. "In other words, it will start to take us the wrong direction for a while. Perhaps we should just venture to cross here. The shadows are getting a little longer, especially next to this cliff. If we hurry, we will minimize the time we can be seen, and again we can camouflage ourselves."

"I'm not sure how well Lily and I can camouflage ourselves as big as we are. It would take a lot of branches, and that would look suspicious," Sarah said.

"Maybe they are still looking for tiny girls and a mouse," Lily said. "They might not notice two little girls on the way home from school."

"Of course they wouldn't," Elwin said. "And that's just what we are going to do. You will pretend that you are girls walking home from school. I will duck down into your pocket, Sarah, until we get across. Just try to stick to the shadows so as to hide yourselves as much as possible and try not to stay on the road too long."

Sarah looked both ways as Mommy had taught them, and then she stepped out onto the road, staying in the shadow of the cliff. They all had a feeling that something was watching them, so they were particularly cautious. Sarah looked all around, but did not see anything suspicious. So she stepped out of the shadow and ran the last few feet of road and into the trees on the opposite side.

"Do you think there was anyone watching?" Lily asked.

"I don't know," Sarah said. "I did not see anyone."

"Of course, we might never know," said Elwin. "A brownie could have been watching while invisible, or perhaps a wood elf watched us while hiding in a tree. Even squirrels or birds could have been enchanted. In cases like these, the first thing they tell you in the elf army is to simply do the best you can with the knowledge that you might be in danger. That's what real bravery is—deciding to do what you set out to even though you know things could turn bad any moment. But then again, there might have been nothing there to watch us."

He made a lot of sense, so they quit worrying and continued on, trying to enjoy the day. In fact, it made them feel a lot better, and they soon dispelled all thoughts of the enemy, at least for the time. The walk was so pleasant, with the leaves changing, the wind blowing, the sun shining, and the path so inviting.

But soon the sun set, the wind turned cold, and the path turned dark and ominous. The friends were nearing the end of their journey back to the witch's cottage, so they began to grow cautious again. At last, they came to a wide field, lying fallow, and across the field they could see the witch's cottage. The girls had approached it from a different angle, but they and Elwin recognized the cottage.

"Let's watch for a moment and see what's afoot," Elwin said.

So they ducked down behind some bushes and sat watching and waiting. The three watched the cottage for what seemed to the girls like a long time. Nothing appeared to move in the nearby fields or in the cottage itself, which remained quiet and dark. Not even birds were flying up to the house. Sarah pulled out some snacks to help pass the time. The friends waited until it was fully dark, and still there was no movement.

"It looks like she's not home," Elwin whispered. "Now's the time to check out the house for the wand. Move over the field as quietly as you can, keeping as low as you can."

Sarah and Lily snuck out across the field, Elwin sitting on Sarah's shoulder. When they crossed from the shoulder-high crops to the woodpile, they stooped down, almost to their waists. Soon, they were approaching the house. Remembering the fairy's warnings, they avoided the vegetable garden with its poisonous herbs and went around to the front door. Sarah peered in the window. It was truly dark inside. Not a lamp was lit, and even the fireplace was cold. It appeared empty. In fact, it appeared as though no one had been there all day.

Sarah opened the door, her heart pounding. Instinctively, she took Lily's hand when she slipped it up to Sarah as they stepped inside. They closed the door quickly, so no one would see them go inside. Then they waited a moment for their eyes to adjust to the darkness, which was as dark as pitch other than in front of the front window.

"Should we light a light?" Sarah whispered, almost breathlessly.

Elwin shook his head, then, putting his mouth into her ear where his whiskers tickled her, he whispered back almost imperceptibly, "Don't talk or make a sound. She may have bugs in the house listening in and reporting everything that's said. I will point the way to the wand, so you can move to it without saying anything."

He pointed across the room to the stairs. Sarah and Lily walked quietly, being careful to avoid the furniture. Elwin pointed up the stairs, so they climbed up, trying not to trip in the dark. He pointed toward the witch's room, and they pushed the door open. It squeaked as it opened, so they just cracked it enough to let them pass. Once they slipped into the room, Elwin pointed toward the wardrobe. They started to move across.

Suddenly, the room lit up like it was on fire. The girls blinked as they tried to get used to the light. Out from behind the bed jumped short little men with ugly, disfigured faces, clawed hands, and pointed ears.

"Goblins!" Elwin squeaked.

There had to be a dozen of them, most of them heavily armed with shields, knives, swords, spears, sticks with nails in them, and other hideous weapons. They were shining a lantern in Sarah's and Lily's faces.

Elwin quickly slid down into Sarah's pocket to avoid being seen.

"Don't move!" a throaty voice commanded from behind them. Sarah looked over her shoulder. Another dozen goblins were coming up the stairs with the largest and ugliest of them leading the way.

"So, thought you would just sneaks around the queen's castle," he grunted. "Trying to spy on her, eh? Well, lucky for us, we spied you first."

"No, we . . ." Sarah began.

"Shut up," the leader said. "Or we will deal with you, orders or no orders. Tie 'em up, boys."

The other goblins pulled out ropes and tied their arms down to their chests and then took out chains and locked them around their waists. They made a horrid racket. How they ever stood in the dark without making a sound, Sarah and Lily would never know.

As the goblins tied them, one of them started to poke Lily and drool. "This one'll make good eating," it said. Lily started to cry.

"None of that," the leader yelled at the other, punching him in the head. "We have our orders. We are to take them alive."

"But she won't need both of them," the little weasel argued. "Leave us the small one to make some stew."

Several of the others seemed to murmur in agreement.

"Now look here," the leader said, grabbing the first one and pushing him into the others. "Do what I say, or you'll pay for it. If I don't kill you first, the witch is sure to turn you into a bunch of rocks, like she did to Garbo when he decided to eat those elves."

In the commotion, Sarah put her head down to her pocket and whispered. "Quick, Elwin, get away while they are not looking. Go get the fairies. It's our only chance."

Elwin did not have to be told twice. He jumped down onto the ropes, slid off onto the floor, and ran up under the bed.

"As for you," said the leader turning to Sarah and Lily. "No use whimpering. We may not be able to kill you, but we can hurt you if you don't do as we say," he added, brandishing a whip.

The goblins finished tying them up and putting gags over their mouths.

"Now, let's not keep the queen waiting. You have an appointment, and that's one I would not want to miss."

He laughed gruffly as he led them away.

14

The Goblin Halls

The goblins led Sarah and Lily out to the barn and into the storeroom. Throwing aside some bags of fertilizer, they opened a trap door in the floor.

"I knew there was something in that storeroom," Sarah said to herself.

Inside the trapdoor was a stairway that circled down deeper and deeper until it disappeared in the darkness. With half a dozen goblins in front of them carrying torches or lanterns, the girls climbed down, down, down until they reached a long hallway, neatly carved and perfectly level. Goblins may be evil, but they can dig.

The hallway continued straight for a long way, and then they came to a series of turns, some left, some right, some sloping up, some down, until Sarah and Lily lost all sense of direction. Several times, the goblin leader would stop and look around, trying to choose the right tunnel. Sarah could only think, if they can't find their way, however are we going to? Still, the goblins continued on. They would go straight, climb some stairs, then turn and open a door. Sometimes they would go through large chambers, which, although Sarah and Lily could not see the walls, their echoing footsteps told them how large the caverns were. After crossing these large, empty spaces, there was always another tunnel at the other side. The goblins passed through many rooms where more goblins lived: bedrooms, dining rooms, armories, and recreation rooms—goblins loved playing darts. These living spaces were very smelly, but luckily the girls did not stay in these. However, mostly there were long, empty hallways and constant shuffling of feet.

At first, the sight of the goblins was nauseating. They looked a little like a cross between pigs, elves, and short little men (they were only around as tall as Sarah). Most had pointed ears, wide upturned noses like a pig, pointed and rotting teeth, and large hands and feet. Each had some kind of deformity—knots on their heads or cheeks, warts, crooked fingers or noses, and so forth. They smelled disgusting, a little of sweat and mud and a little of the rotting food crumbs they left in their unkempt hair and folds in their skin. A whiff of their breath made the girls gag. On top of it all, the goblins were vicious and mean, always hitting, kicking, biting, or insulting each other. They did not behave this way toward the girls, but apparently it was because they were given orders not to "harm or handle" the packages they were told to pick up. As they journeyed on, the girls were able to stand them, but often only by looking away, holding their breaths, and thinking of something pleasant.

After the girls passed the first turn, Sarah realized that if Elwin were to follow, he would not be able to find them through all the twists and turns. So, Sarah decided she needed to leave a sign. She worked her hand around in the ropes until she pulled a small bead bracelet from her wrist, broke the string, and then let the beads fall to the ground one by one each time they passed an intersection. When she had run out of beads, she reached along her dress until she found a tag, and then pulled it off and dropped it. At one point, the goblins let them sit down to rest, and she pulled a gold thread out of one of her socks and let it fall to the ground. At another point, she pulled a hair out with her teeth and dropped it. There might be little left of her clothes or hair when they got to their destination, but it was all she could think of to help the pursuers Sarah hoped would be following soon.

As they walked, Sarah and Lily grew more and more tired. It had been a long day of walking, and it was now long past their bedtime. Their legs were aching, their feet were swollen and numb, they had stitches in their sides, and their heads were confused and cloudy. Still, they went on and on, until it all just seemed a blur of passages and turns and rooms. As they lost all sense of location and time, their journey became more and more like a waking nightmare of being lost.

After the goblins had gone for what seemed like hours, and the girls felt like their little legs could carry them no farther, they came to a stop. While Sarah and Lily sat panting, the leader unlocked a door on one wall. He motioned, and the other goblins threw the girls in and locked the door behind them. It was some kind of vacant storeroom with empty shelves. It was not exactly a jail, but it made a good place for the goblins to lock them for safekeeping. At first, Sarah and Lily lay there afraid to move. Finally, once they realized they were alone and were not being watched—at least not carefully—Sarah wiggled up on her knees and crawled over next to Lily. Lily was lying there with tears running down her cheek. Sarah leaned over until her hand could reach Lily's gag and pulled it down. Then she lay down on the ground and motioned to Lily, who did the same.

"Sarah, I think we are lost. I don't think anyone will ever find us again," Lily sobbed.

"It'll be OK, Lily," Sarah comforted, though she was far from sure herself. They had come a long way in such a short time. But she felt like for Lily's sake she needed to be positive. "Elwin got away, didn't he? And he's going to get the Fairy Queen. She would not let us rot down here.

The fairies will come and get us. At least she will make an attempt."

"But what can we do?" Lily wondered out loud.

"Well," thought Sarah, "First, we need to keep a positive outlook. I think Daddy said he learned in the Army that is the first thing to do in these kinds of situations. Then, we need to look for an opportunity, if not to escape, to gum up the works. Above all, we need to beware of the witch when we get to her, and not give in if she tries to offer us food or nice things or if she threatens us."

"But how can we think positive when so many bad things have happened?" Lily asked.

"Mommy always sings happy songs when she is sad. Maybe we could sing some songs from church or something Mommy sings. Can you remember any songs?"

Lily tried hard to think. "No, I can only think about those evil men."

"Here's one," Sarah said.

She started to sing *Oh, Happy Day*, which was one of her favorites. But Lily did not know all the words. Then she started to sing *Lay Down, My Sweet Baby*, an Appalachian lullaby that their mother had sung to them since they were babies. Lily started to sing along, too. That's when a goblin banged on the door.

"Shut up with that racket," he said until they quieted down.

They lay still for several moments snuggling next to each other. Then Lily began to quietly sing, *Twinkle, Twinkle Little Star*, which was one of her favorites. Sarah joined softly in. After that, they sang, *Away in a Manger*, which, like for most children, was their favorite Christmas carol. As they sang, they thought about home, hearth, and the love of their parents. The songs reminded them that this was just an adventure and that their lives and families waited for them at the end. No matter how dire their situation, this would get better. By the time they finished singing, they felt a lot better, and even Lily had stopped crying.

After a while, one of the goblins brought in some stale and moldy bread and a bowl of water. Even as hungry as they were, neither Sarah nor Lily could stomach the bread, which was black with green fuzz on the crust. Aside from their disgust, they also would not eat it for fear of it being enchanted or poisoned. However, Sarah took some snack food out of her pack, which she still had with her. They nibbled a bit and felt better. Since the girls had run out of water some time ago, they did drink the water the goblins brought, which, although probably not perfectly clean, was at least clear and did not appear dirty or bad.

"We will get out of this mess somehow," Sarah said. "We just have to keep hope alive. Elwin, the fairies, and even the fairy dragon are all on our side and will come looking for us."

"But how will they find us down here?" Lily asked.

"Well, I have been trying to drop signs at every turn, beads, a hair, a thread, anything. If you do the same, it will leave a trail that someone can find. All we will have to do is to wait for someone to follow."

It was not much comfort, but at least Sarah and Lily knew they were doing all they could. They snuggled close to each other and finally fell asleep.

The next morning, the goblins unlocked the door and grabbed their chain, pulling the girls into the hallway. One of the goblins gave them something to drink—some kind of potion that woke them up and made them feel less sore. It burned going down their throat and made them choke and cough, but after a few minutes, Sarah and Lily felt warm and alert.

Within minutes, the goblins were on their way again. It was more of the same—mile after mile of grueling running, constant turning, and, the girls eventually noticed, increasing heat. This was not very noticeable at first, but it was getting warmer, as though they were getting closer to some underground source of heat.

The girls continued to leave signs the best they could, with Lily dropping her own signs, strands of hair, buttons from her shirt, or whatever she could find. After what seemed like many more hours, the hallway finally dumped into a huge cavern. Stalagmites and stalactites decorated the cave like enormous teeth. In the center of the cave were three large bonfires that seemed to reach to the ceiling. This made the hall extremely hot. Dancing around the fires were hundreds of goblins leaping about perversely with pitchforks and spears. Drummers kept a beat going on their drums. On the edges of the hall were tables with whatever nasty food the goblins ate.

The guards started to push their way through the crowd, as the horde of goblins all started gathering around them, gibbering and drooling.

"They have brought food," someone in the crowd shouted. The goblins all started shouting and dancing furiously. The little men pressed in on every side until they started to push the guards down. Several large goblins lifted up Sarah and Lily above their heads.

"What shall we do with them?" one of the goblins shouted.

"Boil 'em!"

"Skin 'em!"

"Roast 'em!"

"Ah, that's it!" another replied. "Tie 'em to a spit, and let's put 'em over the fire."

The goblins pulled out long sticks and pushed them under the ropes behind the girls' backs, and then the goblins hoisted the girls up and carried them toward the fire.

"Wait!" the lead guard shouted as he stood in their way. "These are not for eating. They're for the king."

The other goblins pushed him out of the way. They were just about to put the girls over the fire when a large flash and a puff of smoke appeared on one end of the hall. All of the goblins stopped what they were doing and started to cower. On a raised dais stood an enormously fat goblin with a wide crown on his head and his hands raised.

"What are you doing with my prisoners?" he shouted. "Release them immediately or face my wrath."

The goblins all backed away from Sarah and Lily. The guards pushed their way forward again and reclaimed their prize. They pulled the spits loose and pushed the girls through the crowd toward the king. The king had taken his seat on a throne made from the stalagmites poking up from the ground.

The guards pushed the girls until they stood before the king. The guards seemed to bow politely, but less than enthusiastically than the rabble below.

"Oh, mighty King Grazan, we have brought the two humans as the witch requested," the lead goblin said. "They came to her house, just as she said."

"And what of the mouse?" he asked.

"What mouse?"

"There was supposed to be a mouse with them."

"We saw no mouse. Besides, why should we be concerned with a mouse?"

"It was more than a mouse," the king responded. "It was enchanted, I was told. We may regret your stupidity. In any case, the witch is not here. We will wait until her return."

A goblin from the crowd approached carefully. "If the witch is not here," he asked once he got to the foot of the dais, "Why can't we roast the humans?"

"Hoblob," the king responded. "Do you have a death wish, or are you merely witless? How will you explain their disappearance when the witch returns? She would destroy you instantly, or better yet, turn you into a rabbit and feed you to the dogs. And you wonder why you have never been made a commander."

"But certainly, the witch doesn't need both of the humans," a rather large goblin said, emboldened by Hoblob's complaint. "Why can't we roast just *one* of them? We will even take the little one."

"The witch wanted both alive to question. After she is done with them, then we can cook them any way you want. But not before! Not before!"

"But . . ." one of them started to speak.

"Begone!" the king shouted as he stood and the fire flashed. "I should have *you* roasted up and served for dinner, Gorbub! I have spoken, and I am king!"

They all backed off except the guards.

"Take the humans into my chambers. I will deal with them personally," the king said.

The guards took Sarah and Lily into a large living area, with several small padded chairs. A carpet was on the floor, and there were benches along the walls. Torches hanging off the walls lit the room. Compared to where the girls stayed the night before, it was actually a nice room, aside from the smell. It reeked heavily of goblin. Once they were in the room, all the guards but one left the room.

A few minutes later, the goblin king entered.

"Search through their bags," the king commanded. The goblin guard took out all their food and camping equipment from the bag. He did not open the potion bottle that was with the food, assuming it was just some drink. The guard felt through their extra clothes, but there was nothing particularly suspicious in them. He did not notice the many missing buttons and strings, for all goblin clothes are missing things and are torn and ragged. He also did not find the fairy child. Sarah was glad now that she had left the petrified fairy the size of a pebble. The guard obviously was not looking for anything so small.

"Untie them, and leave us," the king said.

The guard looked at him and started to object.

"Don't be an idiot. They are little girls. I think I can handle two little girls. And besides, where would they go? I'm sure they like this nice room better than roasting over the fire, which is surely what will happen if the others catch them."

The guard obeyed, and left them. Sarah and Lily rubbed their arms where the ropes had bit into them. They looked fearfully at the goblin king as he walked around them looking at them. He bared his pointed teeth, breathing out deeply as though it were winding him just to walk around. His breath was worse than the others, and the girls tried not to breathe in while he was near them. Finally, he sat down in a chair and reached over to a bowl on a table next to it. He started to take something out of the bowl and put it into his mouth. It looked like fat off a piece of ham, but it could have been fish or worms for all they knew.

"Now, what I want to know," started the king, "is why the witch should want you? You are not warriors. You are not sorceresses. You are not elves or fairies. You are just little girls without any apparent magical powers. What makes you so special?"

"Nothing," said Sarah. "I don't know why she has brought us." Of course, she knew that this was not true, but she hoped that the goblin did not know.

"Ah, but I do. You were in her house. So tell me, if there is nothing special about you, why were you in her house, eh?"

"We took a wrong turn and ended up in the cottage. We did not mean to be there at all. I think you must have gotten the wrong people. Perhaps two other humans were coming later—with a mouse, as you said. I mean, we never saw a mouse."

"Hmmm," he said, thoughtfully.

"If I were you, I would send your men back for the right people and let us go. They have probably gone all through that house and are well down the road."

"Perhaps you would like for us to take you back home and tuck you in your beds. Ha, ha. No, we would not take you back to the surface now, even if we had the wrong people. We would just roast you for dinner. Now, what do you say?"

Evidently, the king was either afraid of them causing him trouble, or else he was looking for some kind of information to use against the witch. Perhaps the goblins were afraid of her, too. Mommy always told them that wild animals were usually just as afraid of people as people were of them. The goblins likely did not know a whole lot about people and, since the witch wanted them, he feared they contained some kind of magic. Sarah took a chance that he was afraid of their powers and tried to bluff her way out.

"Look, you had better let us go right now. We have powerful friends who will come looking for us, and then you will be sorry."

"You would dare threaten me?" the king asked. He stood up and started to pull back his hand to hit Sarah, but something kept him from doing it.

"There's definitely something magical. I just can't put my finger on it. Something good is watching over you. Like fairy magic. Ahh! I think I begin to see. So you *are* more than little girls. You are fairy children. You are a threat to her."

So that was it, Sarah thought. The goblin king was looking for a way to get the witch out of his hair. Perhaps she had threatened them, or maybe the king didn't like someone bossing him around. Either way, Sarah might be able to use this to her advantage. She could tell him that they could get rid of the queen if he would let them go.

She was just about to suggest that when the door opened and the head guard walked in. “Mighty One, the witch has arrived.”

“Tie them back up,” the king said as he left the room. Another guard came in and tied Sarah and Lily up tighter than before. Then the goblins left Sarah and Lily waiting for their doom.

15

The Witch

Sarah and Lily waited in the goblin king's quarters for what seemed a long time. The witch was evidently taking her time in coming to see them. At first, Sarah nosed around the room, moving carefully since her arms were tied. There were two other doors leading out of the room. One led out into the main hall and was locked. The other opened into a dining hall with a long table, a dozen chairs, and fancy decorations—a tablecloth, candelabra, centerpiece, and fancy flatware. It was obviously not for the goblins, for they were not cultured enough to have such decorations. It must be for the witch or the elves and humans that served her, Sarah thought. A door led from that room into a kitchen and other chambers. Sarah could see through a round window on the door, but when she tried to open it, it was locked. So Sarah and Lily returned to the first room and sat down on chairs the best they could to wait.

After many more minutes, the witch came in. She was as the girls had seen her at her cottage—a short old lady with white hair up in a bun. She looked a little like someone's grandmother. Yet, despite her seeming old age, she moved rapidly across the room, as though she were young and determined. The witch could hide her appearance, but not her personality or energy, Sarah thought. Then, throwing her cloak over a chair, she turned to them.

"Ah, so these are the trespassers in my house," the witch said in a kind old voice, laughing sweetly. Sarah and Lily were taken aback. They expected a mean old hag, but the witch looked and acted nice.

The witch looked through their bags, noting the potion. Then she walked around them, looking them over much as the goblin king had.

"Pretty little girls. Now, what were two humans doing in my house?"

Sarah cleared her throat. "As we told your goblin friend, we just took a wrong turn. You must be looking for someone else." Sarah hoped that the witch would take notice that the goblin king had already interrogated them, but she did not bat an eye.

The witch looked at them kindly. "Well, first of all, the goblins are not my friends. They have sort of demanded my service, and I really just put up with them—a necessary evil, one might say. As for your being in my house, you really do not need to deny it. My spies knew you were coming and followed you most of the way there."

Lily started to feel like she should just admit everything, but Sarah gave her a look before she opened her mouth, a look that meant she should not talk, so she didn't. Luckily, the fairies had warned them that the witch could trick people into talking. From what the witch said, she had only watched them "coming" to her house, not going from it. Sarah hoped this meant that the witch knew nothing of their specific mission, and she did not want to reveal anything more.

"I could have just as easily transformed you while you were in my house. The reason I had you brought here," the witch continued, "is because I want to know why you broke into my house. I know you are sorceresses of sorts—you have changed sizes and you are consorting with animals. So, were you there to test your magic against mine? Were you thrill-seekers wanting to see if what they say about the old lady is true? Or did someone put you up to it?"

Sarah and Lily stayed silent.

"Very well. You both look hungry," the witch said, going into the dining room. A plate had been set out for her with fruit and some bread, which she brought back with her into the living area. She sat down and started eating some grapes. "Perhaps you would like some food?"

Lily nodded. It had, after all, been more than a day since their last meal.

"Very well. If you cooperate, I will treat you to a feast. What would you like? Chicken? Grapes? Bread and butter? Some milk and chocolate? Anything you want, provided you tell me what I want to know."

Although Sarah and Lily were both hungry, they had already encountered the effects of fairy food, so they knew not to accept her offer. The girls resisted the temptation, however much it hurt to remain hungry when food was so close.

"No thank you," said Sarah. "We will not eat your enchanted food."

The witch laughed. "You are such smart girls," she said. "I see you are too smart to fall for a trick like that. All right. Then I will cut you and torture you until you tell me."

Her eyes flashed as she pulled a knife out from her belt and started to walk toward the girls with an evil smile. She held out the knife to their necks as though she were going to try to cut them. Lily was a little worried, but Sarah knew that she would not harm them until she got the information she wanted. The witch was bluffing again.

"So you are not afraid?" the witch said. "You must be under the protection of something. Don't deny it. I can sense these things. There is some power that you have. Well, then, call on your powers to protect you. Use your magic. Try to keep me from harming you. Turn me into something. Put up a force field. Call on your familiars."

The girls did nothing. Sarah thought she was probably just trying to get them to reveal the powers she thought they had. If Sarah had tried to call on the fairies at that time, they might have appeared, but it would have given away their mission and everything. She would not sell them out just to protect herself. No, it was better to do nothing.

"I guess you will have to kill us, then," Sarah said.

The witch looked at them, then backed up and stuck the knife onto a nearby table, so that the threat of using it was never far removed.

"I see that you are not only smart, but wise. Very well. Let me make you another offer. I have watched you and am impressed by how you have handled yourselves. You have many gifts, not least your intelligence, bravery, and a little magical power. I could use your help. You see, the goblins are not very trustworthy or bright and make poor servants. I know you tried to outwit my brownie at the lake, so you know that they are much too flippant to be trusted for important missions. Most of the humans that help me don't understand about magic. You could be my chief servants. Perhaps I could make you duchesses with power over many. Or if you prefer, you could be my apprentices, learn all about my magic and become powerful witches like me. All you have to do is agree to help me and put your trust in me."

Again, the girls knew that the witch was probably just bluffing, but it was appealing. Sarah liked being in control, almost to the point of being bossy. It would be nice to tell those goblins and men what to do. For Lily, the appeal was getting back at those goblins that wanted to eat them by making them wait on her. And then there was the idea of learning magic. Sarah had read enough books to be intrigued by the idea of learning magic. But the girls had seen the sort of magic the witch knew—turning people into things, killing, destroying, and deceiving. They wanted no part of that kind of life. Besides, the Fairy Queen had already made them princesses, and in her kingdom, people did what you said because they loved and respected you, not because they were afraid of you. That's what Sarah and Lily really wanted, for people to love them.

"We don't want to be friends with anyone whose friends are goblins," Lily said.

"And we would not serve you even if you were a queen and in control of all you say you are," Sarah added.

"Ah, but you see, I am. I am actually a queen with many servants. I only pretend to be an old lady."

The witch backed up a step and waved her hands in front of herself, and with a flash of light and some smoke, the old lady that had been standing before them disappeared. In her place was a tall, young elf princess with black hair. She wore a silver crown, a fine velvet robe, and a necklace with a black stone that swirled with many colors. Her deep black eyes were proud and cruel, her eyebrows as pointed as her ears. In her face was a coldness you might see from bloodthirsty army commanders. She was obviously a woman who was used to commanding.

"You are no queen, no matter how you are dressed," Sarah said. "It takes more than fancy clothes and a crown to be queen."

"But do you not see how powerful I am? I have hundreds of servants, and I would have thousands more. I am the rightful ruler of many peoples—elves, brownies, sprites, and more. With them behind me, I could become the ruler of all the peoples in this country. None could resist me. If it were not for a little upstart, I would be ruling them already."

"You mean the Fairy Queen," Sarah blurted out, angry that the witch had insulted her friend. She saw the change in the witch's expression and knew she had made a mistake.

"Ah, you know the little tramp? That reveals a lot. So, you are her servants? Ha, ha, ha. There is no use in pretending. You have revealed all. Were you spying for her like the other little fairies she sent into my kingdom? Well, you shall soon meet the same end—turned into mice and fed to my cat."

The witch reached to her side. From a sash around her waist hung a slender silver rod inlaid with ivory. It looked a little scepter, but Sarah and Lily guessed this was the very wand they had been seeking. They stared at it as she moved. The witch followed their eyes, and suddenly understood even more.

"I see. You are interested in my wand. Did you want to take it for yourselves? Many a sorceress has tried to steal my wand, so you would not be the first. Or did that fairy woman want you to steal it? She must be trying to rescue all those fairies. Maybe it is the mouse I heard about. He must be one of the fairies I fed to my cat. My old puss must be getting old to let some mice get away. Well, it makes no matter. You will now face your doom."

She held up her wand, preparing to turn them into something.

"What shall it be? Firewood to burn in the fire? Or stones to line my garden? Or maybe I will turn you into mice like your friend."

Then, the witch paused and an evil smile crossed her face. "No, I do not think I will use the wand on you. You do not even deserve that much of a chance. Instead, you will stay for dinner—with the goblins, that is. They have asked for you, and I will let them cook you for breakfast. First, they will skin you, then fry you, or perhaps just stick you on a spit and roast you over the fire. Of course, if you tell me all—why she sent you, what you found out, what were your plans—I might change my mind and allow you to live. Yes, I can be that generous. I will let you ponder that while the goblins stoke their fires."

She turned and withdrew into the dining room and shut the door.

"Do you think she would let us go?" Lily asked.

"Not on your life," said Sarah. "She is just bluffing again. She wants us to tell her everything, then she will feed us to the goblins anyway."

"Well, what can we do?"

Sarah tried to think, but the image of the goblins skinning them kept coming into her mind. "I don't know, Lily. I just don't know."

16

Lily Comes Through

Sarah and Lily stood tied up alone in the goblin king's chambers, waiting on their death to come at any moment. Just outside, the goblins were waiting to cook them for breakfast. In the next room, the witch was waiting to turn them into something if they tried to escape. It was a bleak future indeed.

"Do you have a plan, yet?" Lily asked.

"No. Nothing yet. There appears to be no way out unless either we barge through the goblins or past the witch. Either choice would mean certain death. And besides, we are both tied up tight. We might have a chance, if only one of us could get loose," Sarah said.

"You mean like this," Lily said. Lily pulled her hands out of the loops that were supposed to tie her down.

"You mean you could do that all the time?" Sarah asked.

Lily shrugged. "I don't know. I never tried."

It has long been said that little children are the most difficult to tie up, perhaps because they are so much smaller than any rope that might hold them, or perhaps because being young they are still limber enough that they can contort themselves into unlikely positions to get their hands free. Or perhaps in this case, it was because goblins were not very smart and did not tie her up in a way that small hands cannot escape.

"Good!" Sarah said. "Get all the way out, and then try to untie me."

Lily wiggled until the ropes that held her arms fell to the floor. Then she reached down and pulled on the ropes that held her feet while shuffling her feet back and forth. Soon, Lily was able to pull her feet free by taking off her shoes, which she put on again as soon as she had freed herself. At once, she moved to Sarah to try to untie her, but she could not reach the knot. So Lily stood on a chair and had Sarah back up to her. She tugged and pulled and twisted and even bit, but she could not get the knot on Sarah's rope to loosen.

"Never mind, Lily," Sarah said. "We are going to run out of time. You will have to save us all by yourself. You need to get the wand from the witch. She is in the next room eating. You must try to sneak in and get it."

Lily was wide-eyed with fear. "But she will see me and turn me into a frog or something."

"Not if you are sneaky. Pretend it's a game of hide and seek. Stay out of sight. You could hide under the table. Crawl as quietly as you can. When you get close to her, reach up and get the wand from her belt without pulling on her clothes. Then crawl back."

Lily started to object again, but Sarah only said, "Look, I know it's scary, but one of us has to do it or else we're finished, and I can't do it because I am tied up and cannot get loose."

Lily nodded. She knew that she was the one who had to act, even though she was scared. She went over to the door to the dining room and looked through the keyhole. Lily could see the witch sitting at the table at the far end of the room, eating and drinking while she bellowed out orders to goblins that were coming and going from the other door that went into a kitchen. The edge of the tablecloth was only a few feet from the door where Lily stood. She could do this, she told herself. She could crack the door and get under the table without being seen.

Lily got down on her hands and knees and quietly cracked the door open. It was the riskiest moment, but the witch seemed distracted, so perhaps she would not see. Lily crawled quietly through and shut the door behind her before anyone saw. Then she quickly but quietly crawled under the tablecloth, which came down almost to the ground.

Lily crawled along under the table making no sound, her heart pounding like thunder. She carefully navigated the way over the large table legs that came down in the center of the table so that she neither rocked the table nor exposed herself from under the tablecloth. She continued to crawl along until she was right in front of the witch.

The witch had continued to bark orders to the goblins in between bites of food and gulps of drink: "Send the spies out into the forest. The fairies must be on the move." "What do you mean the patrol by the lake has not reported in?" "This chicken is dry. Cook me another, and this time get it right." "Tell those miserable brownies they had better bring every man they have." Of course, Lily was so intent on getting to the witch, she hardly paid attention, though it seemed that there was a lot of activity, like the witch was preparing for a war.

Lily watched the witch's feet as she continued to eat and yell. Occasionally, the witch would sit upright, but most of the time, she reclined slightly in her chair. The tablecloth was draped across the witch's knees, but Lily could see her belt just past the tablecloth if she positioned herself just right. Lily inched herself forward until the wand was in plain view hanging down from the sash around the witch's waist. It appeared there was a hook hanging from the belt on which the wand was hung by a leather strap. Lily reached forward and gently lifted the wand off the hook. She had it, and the witch had not felt or seen a thing! Lily carefully started to inch her way back under the table.

That's when Lily saw something else. It was the buckle to the witch's sash. She called it a buckle, but it was a perfect oval stone, and the colors reminded her of something—pink with purple swirls. They reminded her of the fairy dragon. Could it be the egg? It certainly was shaped like an egg, even though it was hidden behind a silver buckle. Lily thought back and remembered the promise they had made to the fairy dragon. Should she risk getting the egg? She felt she had to try to keep her promise. But she did not know whether she could reach it without the witch seeing her since the buckle was not under the tablecloth.

Just when she was about to try for it, the witch leaned forward across the table to yell at some hapless goblin that came in the room. The witch scooted forward on the chair until her waist was pressed against the table. Thank-you, Lily thought. It was just the gift she needed. Lily pulled up the tablecloth and carefully unhooked the buckle, gently pulling the entire sash down under the table. The buckle had a clasp on the back that grabbed the sash. All she had to do was push on a lever and the buckle came free. She dropped the sash and started to crawl along under the table. Soon she was at the end close to the door waiting for the right moment to push it open and crawl back to Sarah.

The witch suddenly grew quiet. Lily waited for what seemed an eternity. She began to wonder what happened to the witch. Perhaps she was falling asleep. So, Lily quietly slipped her head above the table, and there the witch was sitting and staring into space, deep in some meditation. Lily pulled her head quickly down. Should she take the risk of opening the door? She knew any moment the witch would discover the theft of her wand and belt buckle. If not that, one of the goblins coming in and out of the room might spot Lily sitting at the end of the table. She had to take the chance. Lily slowly opened the door just a crack and had just started to squeeze her way through. That was when all kinds of devilry broke out.

First the witch shouted, "The door!" Then as if by magic, the door slammed shut. Lily just barely got her head back in without it being pinched in the door. Lily started to crawl under the table again.

"You might as well stand up, thief," the witch said. Apparently, she had noticed her missing belt and wand. Little did Lily know that she had reached for her wand hoping to turn the intruder into something and only then noticed her belt was missing.

Lily waited, hoping maybe the witch would be distracted or not see her. She wished she could crawl under a rock. But instead, the witch stood up and started to slowly move around the table toward the door. Knowing that she would soon be discovered no matter what she did, Lily made the best of the situation, pushed the wand under her belt and shirt behind her back, and slowly stood up. There was the witch, her evil sneer showing her contempt.

"Oh, it's you. Come here, you little beggar!"

At first, Lily did not move, although whether it was out of defiance or fear she could never quite say.

"Come here or I will feed you to the goblins right now!"

Lily finally started to move toward her, but on the opposite side of the table. She kept trying to think of something, anything. Lily knew she had to stay calm and think.

"Now you are going to pay for your insolence. I will turn you into something particularly nasty, like the nasty food that the goblins eat. Now, give me my wand."

Lily held up her hands, as if to say she did not have them. She was still too afraid to speak.

"Where is it, you little crumb? You get my wand immediately, or I will show you no mercy."

Lily put her hand on the table, thinking about whether she should surrender the wand to save her life. That's when she noticed a cup of wine sitting only inches from her hand. Just past the cup stood the candelabra in the table centerpiece. It provided the only light in the room. She saw what could be her only chance. She grabbed the cup and threw the wine at the candelabra, extinguishing the candles. The room plunged into darkness. Before anyone could blink, Lily dropped down and slid up under the table again.

"Aaagghh," the witch yelled, leaning across the table. The witch grabbed for her, but missed and fell over the table, grasping about with her hands hoping to touch Lily as she scurried about the floor. Immediately after the witch screamed, the door into the other room opened, allowing a crack of light to fall across the table, and half a dozen little bare goblin feet came through the door.

"Find that little girl! She's in here somewhere," the witch commanded.

The goblins began running here and there, grabbing and pushing, bumping into the table and chairs and each other. They searched blindly in the room, groping wildly, not knowing what was what. As they grabbed in the dark, they began knocking things over. Soon the candelabra, all the dishes, and everything else on the table were crashing to the floor. The little pieces of plates were crunching loudly, which of course led to screaming as the shards poked into the goblins' bare feet. As she sat under the table, Lily was grateful that the goblins were so thick. All of that racket was a perfect distraction to cover Lily's escape.

"We've got her! We've got her!" two of the goblins yelled, grabbing hold of someone in the dark.

"You've got me! Drat, you fools!" the witch yelled. "Let go and find her!"

The goblins let go and continued their search. Lily heard them lift up the tablecloth and reach up under the table. It would only a few minutes more until they found her.

While all this commotion was going on, Lily crawled like lightning under the table toward the door. As they continued to argue and bump into one another, she cracked the door open and flew through it, closing it quietly behind her.

Sarah was waiting there for her, still trying to work her ropes free with her hands.

"What happened? Did the witch find you? What is all that noise? How did you get away? Did you get the wand?"

Lily held up the wand in answer to her last question; the rest she would have to answer later. Then she started to pull on Sarah's ropes. "Quick, Sarah! You have to get loose. The witch will come any moment."

Lily pushed the wand under the ropes and used it as leverage to stretch the rope until Sarah finally got a hand loose. Then it was only a few seconds more, and her ropes were off, too. Sarah grabbed the wand.

Lily was exactly right. The witch had seen the light from the cracked door as it had opened, and, although she did not see Lily crawl through, she knew that Lily had fled back to her sister. Almost as soon as Sarah was free of the ropes, the door crashed open with a mighty force, as though some magic had blown it apart. There stood the witch in the doorway in front of them, arms wide open as though she were about to bring the room down. The witch saw the girls immediately and started to chant some incantation.

The witch's eyes flashed with intense hatred for those two little girls who had caused her more trouble than an army of elves and fairies. They had stolen her most prized possession and the greatest source of her power—her wand. They had outwitted her goblins and her brownies. They had fooled her and made a mockery of her attempts to be merciful toward them. Now they would pay with their lives.

17

An Old Enemy

The witch stood before Sarah and Lily in the doorway of the dark dining room from which Lily had just escaped. The explosion had cracked the door, which was now hanging off its hinges. The goblins were still fumbling in the dark behind her searching for Lily. The witch strolled into the room through a cloud of smoke facing off the two girls. Sarah stood facing the door with the witch's wand in her hand. Lily stood hiding behind her.

"Give me the wand!" the witch yelled. The girls did nothing, for they were very afraid. One always thinks of the best thing to say or do after the fact, and this was certainly the case with Sarah and Lily facing such terrible danger. "Very well, I will destroy you," the witch continued. "Perhaps you would like some fire?"

The witch began to conjure. Words of some strange language rolled off her tongue. As she spoke, her hand turned red and began to glow as flames leapt up among her fingers.

Sarah and Lily jumped behind a couch in the nick of time. The witch threw the fire across the room and hit the couch, which instantly leapt into flames. The smoke obscured their view of the witch, and Sarah feared that she was sneaking around behind them. So, Sarah stood up and pulled out the wand.

Perhaps I can use the wand to turn the witch into something, Sarah thought. She assumed that a wand was like a gun—all you had to do was point it at something and fire. She ran out from behind the couch, Lily trailing after her. Once she was in the clear, Sarah pulled out the wand and pointed it at the witch, who had remained motionless while she cast her spell.

"Oh, are you going to turn me into something, dear?" the witch said, laughing. "What will you turn me into? A mouse? A goblin? Or perhaps something even smaller, like a flea."

"That's right," Sarah said. "Or perhaps I should turn you into stone like what you did to all those poor little fairies. It would only be what you deserved for the evil that you have caused."

Sarah moved the wand in a circle, snapping her wrist as she had seen the witch use it. Some kind of electricity or power jumped out of the wand, shocking Sarah dreadfully. Her hand went limp, and the wand fell out of her hand onto the floor. It was a move that Sarah regretted for a long time to come. She later learned that the devices of the enemy are not to be used, whether magic or hate or fear. Anything she tried with the wand would have only caused more trouble, just as trying to scare someone into doing what you want will always hurt people you do not intend. The witch, seeing Sarah grab her arm, started to laugh.

"Ha, ha, ha. Thought you were powerful enough to use my wand, eh? Stupid girl! You were pointing it the wrong way. It takes more than a little fairy dust to work real magic. Now, let me show you power at work."

The witch stepped forward and reached for the wand. Sarah stood helplessly watching her, still nursing her numb hand. The witch grabbed the wand and stood up. Sarah felt the blood rushing back into her hand as a tingling sensation in her fingers let her know that it was not permanently damaged.

"Now, I will turn you into something for real. Ah, I have it—a pig for the goblins to roast on the fire. This time I will not wait and give you the chance to discomfort me more."

The witch began chanting in some strange language again. But this time, she would not complete her spell. Sarah ran forward and grabbed the wand near the bottom, trying to pull it out of the witch's hand. With two sets of hands on the wand, it did not know who its master was, and hence the two sets of wills and minds commanding it cancelled each other out. The witch's magic did not work while Sarah was grabbing the wand.

Although the witch was stronger and tougher than her youth and beauty revealed, she was still an elf. She was only a little taller than Sarah herself—about four and a half to five feet tall. And she was very petite with little strength, probably from posing as a harmless old lady for so many years. Sarah, meanwhile, was tall for her age and very active. They were a close match, with the witch having only a small advantage in the struggle. They fought back and forth for several minutes. First, Sarah surprised the witch by grabbing the wand and nearly yanking it out of her hand. Then the witch yanked back, trying to use her slight edge in height as an advantage to knock Sarah off her feet. But Sarah planted her feet and yanked back. The witch tried twisting her hands to make Sarah let go, but Sarah held on for dear life. Even when she lost her balance once, she managed to hold on until she could regain her feet. But she knew that the witch had more stamina and would eventually wear her down.

As Sarah fought with the witch, Lily stood watching, scared to move. Out of habit, she stuck her hand in her pocket, and discovered a smooth, cold object. She pulled it out. It was the witch's belt buckle. She looked again at the pink oval stone with purple swirls—it had to be the dragon's egg! She pushed on the stone until it popped out of the silver buckle. There it was: an egg if she had ever seen one.

Across the room, several goblins came out of the dark to watch the witch that they feared and called master now struggling with a human child. Instead of intervening, they simply stood watching, waiting for the outcome and hoping that maybe this time the witch had met her match. If she lost, they could proceed with doing what they wanted with the prisoners. If she won, they could always rush in to take them prisoner again as though they had been waiting for an opportunity all along.

Sarah continued to fight to wrench the wand out of the witch's hands until the witch pulled a dirty move. She dropped to the ground on her back, flipping Sarah over her with her feet. Still, Sarah managed keep her hold right until the moment she hit the ground. At that instant, her weight falling with her fingers wrapped around the wand stripped it from both their hands, sending it flying across the room and under a coffee table and chair next to the burning couch.

Both Sarah and the witch got up and bolted in the direction they saw the wand fly. As Sarah ran past Lily, Lily handed Sarah the egg.

"The egg, Sarah! The fairy dragon's egg! Remember what it said?"

Sarah grabbed the egg as the witch got down on her hands and knees looking for the wand under chairs and tables.

"Ah-hah," yelled the witch as she stood up with the wand in her hand.

"T'srak L'agwenda, T'srak L'agwenda, T'srak L'agwenda!" Sarah shouted at the top of her lungs.

The witch stopped what she was doing, as the dragon's name seemed to echo across time and space. The air suddenly started to ripple like heat coming off a paved road. As the air stabilized, a tiny pink sphere appeared over their heads, growing larger and larger as it moved toward the floor. It grew until it was about five feet across, and then it started to fade, leaving a small lizard figure in its midst. The fairy dragon had come!

As soon as it appeared, the dragon looked at Sarah holding the egg, and, realizing its precious offspring was safe, flew at the witch before she had time to use the wand. The dragon rushed at the witch, breathing fire on her hands, which made her drop the wand. The witch tried to recover it, but the dragon moved on top of it. The thing was not very big now—about the size of a small dog—but flying made it seem a lot bigger because it had a much wider wing span. The witch backed away, knowing that even a dragon this size was more than her match. While the dragon kept the witch busy, Lily ran up and grabbed the wand again.

"T'srak L'agwenda," the witch said. "You fool. How dare you interfere with my plans. I will destroy your egg if you come a step closer."

The dragon smiled and flew toward the witch. Fiara reached down toward her belt, and only then remembered that it had been stolen. She grimaced across the room at Sarah, who still held the egg aloft.

"Fiara, you wicked elf witch. The egg is mine again, thanks to these human children. Now, you no longer have power over me."

"It is not yours yet," the witch said, bolting around the dragon toward Sarah.

Sarah moved to keep the dragon between them. The witch reversed herself and ran the other way, but Sarah also changed directions. T'srak roared and breathed out fire, forcing the witch to stop. Then, it backed up toward Sarah and reached a claw behind it. Sarah put the egg in its clawed hand. The dragon took it, and with a motion of its hand, used its own magic to send the egg to some secret place far out of harm's way.

"You may have won the egg back, but you know very well I have other powers. You will be sorry you challenged me," the witch said.

The dragon spread its wings and flew toward the witch with colors swirling. But the witch was prepared and threw up her cloak before her eyes. The witch began to conjure once again, but this time she faced an angry dragon, not two small children. The dragon flew toward the witch, grabbing her cloak with its claws and yanking her off balance, ruining her spell. So far, it was a pretty even match.

The witch fell over into a chair, and saw next to her the long knife sticking upright in an end table, where she had left it. She reached over and yanked it out, holding it in front of her, guarding herself. As the dragon swooped down again with its wings swirling, Fiara stabbed its wings, tearing one of them and sending the dragon to the ground to break its spell. However, this did not slow the serpent at all. Instead T'srak half crawled and half slithered until it wrapped around the witch's leg, entangling her arm and the knife in its tail. Fiara tried to pull the knife free with her other hand, but the dragon held tight. Back and forth they went, but the dragon was the stronger of the two, and the knife soon fell harmlessly to the floor.

The witch pulled free, taking several steps back.

"Now we will truly test your strength," the witch said. She quickly completed a chant, and a cloud of smoke appeared. Out of the smoke came two hands that started to reach toward the dragon. The dragon lifted its arms and wings, and a purple rope appeared that wrapped around the hands. Then as quickly as the hands appeared, the apparitions faded leaving nothing but a little mist in the air.

"You have grown powerful," the dragon said. "But not powerful enough. I am a fairy dragon, not some servant of evil you can control. You cannot destroy me, and you know it."

"Perhaps not," the witch said. "But I can destroy those whom you would protect. You can resist magic, but you are helpless against the forces of nature."

The witch began to conjure again as wind swept the room. Dark storm clouds began to form over the witch's head and lighting began to spark from her hands and from the clouds. The wind quickly became gale strength, so that Sarah and Lily had to lean forward to keep from being pushed over. The goblins watching near the door backed out of the room, so that only their peering eyes could still be seen in the dark dining hall. The dragon made itself low to the ground so as not to be blown away. Soon the wind became hurricane strength, as Sarah and Lily were pushed back. Sarah tried grabbing a chair, but the chair blew away and crashed against the wall. The wind forced Sarah and Lily into a corner until they could not move.

The clouds over the witch's head continued to darken the room until the girls could see nothing but the witch and the dragon and then only dimly when lightning struck. The witch pointed her hands toward the girls. Lightning streaked from the cloud, striking the couch in front of Sarah and Lily. The couch burst into flames again. Another strike like that, and they would be dead. Because of the wind, the girls could barely move, making them easy targets.

The dragon was pressed down by the wind. However, instead of being dismayed by the witch's fury, it rushed straight into danger, slithering on the floor toward the witch. Lightning crashed out of the clouds toward the dragon, but missed it, leaving a black mark on the floor. The witch did not seem to notice and was staring intently at the girls. Sarah and Lily looked up and could see lightning building up in the clouds as the clouds ionized. They knew lightning would strike them again in only a few seconds.

The dragon crawled to the foot of the witch. Once out of the wind, it wrapped itself around the witch again. This time, however, there was no struggle as the witch concentrated on destroying Sarah and Lily and ignored the dragon. Very slowly, the witch and dragon began to be surrounded by a pink cloud. The cloud hardened into a sphere. The sphere grew until the witch and the dragon were engulfed by it. The sphere began to fly up toward the ceiling, taking them with it. The sphere become smaller and smaller until both witch and dragon disappeared.

Within minutes of the witch disappearing, the wind slowed and the storm clouds began to dissipate. The unnatural darkness began to lift. In another few minutes, the room was calm. Were it not for the furniture and trash blown about the room, one would have never known that the room had been the site of the first underground hurricane. The goblins watching on the edge of the room suddenly became quite frightened and fled back into the darkness to some other hall.

The danger of the witch was gone, but Sarah and Lily were not out of the woods by any stretch. They were still lost and alone in the goblin halls, and the goblins were still waiting in the next room to roast them alive.

18

The Battle of Goblin Hall

The witch had disappeared with the fairy dragon, never to be heard from again. Neither Sarah nor Lily nor anyone else ever found out what exactly happened to her. Some of the witch's servants said that she escaped, and they waited for many years for the witch to show up again, but she never did. Sarah and Lily assumed that the dragon destroyed the witch somewhere alone in the forest, for they later heard that the dragon was living in her old haunts in the mushroom patch, but they never had a chance to inquire. All the girls knew was that the dragon had her egg and that the witch was gone.

At that moment, however, Sarah and Lily could not worry about the witch. They had to figure how to get past the horde of goblins to find their way back up to the surface and back to their home. They knew the goblins were waiting right outside the door, and at any moment, they would become suspicious of not having heard from the witch. Then the goblins would know everything that had happened and take Sarah and Lily to roast on their fire.

"There are hundreds of goblins out there," Sarah said. "We are not warriors and have no chance of overpowering the goblins or trying to outrun them, especially since they outnumber us. And we have no magic to help us other than being friends with fairies. We will have to sneak out. Can you think of a way to get past them without them knowing it was us?"

Lily shook her head. "Maybe a smoke screen, but the only fire big enough to make that much smoke is in their hall."

"Perhaps we can dress up like the witch and try to make it out of the hall," Sarah said. "The goblins would not mess with her. They are scared of her."

"But Sarah, when she was dressed as an old lady, she was taller than either one of us," Lily said.

"You could sit on my shoulders, and we could put on her cloak, the one she wore and left on that chair. It would only fool the goblins if they didn't get too close or try pulling the cloak off, but my bet is they won't. They would be too frightened of the witch to go near. In any case, it's either that or go out and face them alone."

Since neither of the girls liked that idea, they decided to try dressing up like the witch. If caught, they would be no worse off than they were stuck inside that room. They might even be able to make a run for it if they could get close enough to the exit.

The girls got together their things, which the goblins had left on the ground when they had searched their packs. They repacked their clothes, their backpacks, the potion and remaining food, the rope, the flashlights, and their camping gear. The wand Sarah placed in her belt under her shirt to hide it. Then Lily climbed up on Sarah's shoulders. Putting the witch's cloak over their heads, they carefully hid their packs so that the bags did not stick out too far. Lily pulled the hood over her head so that nothing of her face could be seen. Sarah pulled the sleeves together so that it looked like the witch had her hands clasped in front of her. To allow Sarah to be able to see to guide them out of the goblin hall, she left a small gap open in the front of the cloak by not buttoning it up tightly. Finally, they were ready for their charade.

Sarah walked up to the door leading from the king's chambers and opened it. The goblin guards near the door came to attention and did not look at them as they left. The goblin crowd nearest the door began to back away. Apparently, the witch had burned or transformed enough of them that they now avoided her when she came into the room. It was just as Sarah guessed. Everything was working out fine.

Sarah kept to the edge of the hall, making her way around the bonfires where the goblins continued to dance and gibber. She moved gradually to the door leading back out into the corridor on the far side of the fire. The goblins continued to get out of her way and bow in respect as she passed. Only two dozen yards or so to go, and the girls would make it out.

Now, the old goblin king was still in the room, but being busy feasting and telling stories, he did not see Sarah and Lily come through the door. It was only out of chance that he looked up from his meal and saw what looked like the witch making her way across the hall.

"Ah, there is the witch, now. See, and you little squealers said that a dragon had destroyed her. Preposterous," the king said loudly to one of his companions. Evidently, the goblins that had waited on the witch had gotten away and tried to tell others what had happened.

"Witch Queen!" he shouted to Sarah and Lily. "Queen Fiara! Come, where are you going? We must confer."

Sarah continued to move toward the door. A few more yards, and they would be out of the great hall. Then, the goblin king could not stop them. They would be able to run down the hallway and hide in one of the rooms they saw on their way in. They just needed to ignore him and continue to move.

"Queen!" he shouted again, getting up from his table and striding across the room. Sarah kept moving. Only a dozen more yards to go, and they would be out the door. He moved quickly for a fat old goblin. He was gaining on them. The door was within sight. There was a guard on either side with large halberds or axes on long poles. Just past the guards, the hallway disappeared into the dark. A few more feet, and they would be out.

"Queen, we must discuss the war," he said, coming up right behind them. As he approached, he stepped on their cloak, which dragged the ground. The cloak pulled off Lily's head. Her blond hair suddenly became visible. The goblins all gasped.

"Stop them!" the king screamed.

The two guards crossed the axes in front of the door, blocking the way. Lily jumped down, throwing off the cloak. Both of the girls dropped to their hands and knees and started to crawl under the guards' legs. But hands grabbed their feet and pulled them back. Soon, they were hoisted up and plopped down in front of the king again.

"So, thought you could fool everyone!" the king said. "I knew there was something wrong when you did not stop when I called. Although the witch and I do not always get along well, she would never leave on the eve of a battle without consulting me.

"Well, now, if you are running out using the witch's cloak, it can only mean that the witch is gone. Since she would not have left of her own freewill with the two of you still alive and untransformed, it can only mean you defeated her somehow. Or perhaps it is as Graza said, and a dragon killed her. In either case, that means we don't have to worry about her anymore."

Sarah suddenly broke free and ran over to the fire, kicking over a log and stirring cinders and smoke into the air. She started to pull out the wand. After her last experience, she would not use it, but she thought it would certainly frighten the goblins and possibly make them leave her alone. In the end, she decided not to try out of fear that the goblins might try to take the wand from her or that she might lose it and the chance to rescue the fairy child.

"I destroyed the witch with fire!" Sarah said. "And I will destroy you, too, if you do not let us go our way. You have already delayed us long enough."

The goblins started to back away, all except the king. He only started to laugh, a mean, ugly laugh.

"You fooled us once. But I know better. You did not destroy the guards when they captured you. And you did not destroy me. I don't know exactly what happened to the witch, but I doubt you had anything to do with it. So, if you indeed have powers, go ahead and use them. Throw fire at me. Turn me into something."

He laughed again when Sarah could do nothing. The guards pushed in toward her and grabbed her. Another group surrounded Lily a few feet away.

"Now," the king said, "You may take them and roast them."

The goblins began to dance and yell and drool, as they got excited again. They started to lead them off in different directions, one toward each of the large bon fires in the room.

"Sarah!" Lily yelled as the goblins pulled them apart. She grabbed Sarah's backpack, but the goblins continued to pull on Sarah, stripping the pack off her in the process. Lily kept hold of the pack as they were separated. Still, she reached for Sarah, crying and screaming for her sister.

"Bring in the rope and spits," one goblin called.

"Wait, we must skin 'em," another said. Sarah cringed at the thought.

"No, leave the skin on 'em," said a third. "It will seal the juices in."

They brought out the rope and started to tie Sarah up. Lily could see a goblin with rope approaching and could just make out over the heads of the crowd the two long poles the goblins would tie them onto while turning them over the fire.

Lily had to do something. She looked down at Sarah's backpack. The wand was not there. She guessed that Sarah had it. Was there anything else that might help? She opened the top and looked inside. There on the top was the flask with the potion in it. Quickly, before anyone had noticed what she had done, she pulled it out, took off the cap, and poured some down her throat.

Oh, how it gagged Lily. It was hideous-tasting. She coughed and spat, trying to get the taste out of her mouth. As Lily looked down at her toes, she noticed that they already seemed to be getting farther and farther away. Then, she felt something bump her head. She looked up. It was the ceiling of that enormous cavern. She looked down, and below her, she saw the goblins running to and fro like little dolls that had come to life.

The goblins, meanwhile, looked up at this giant, and started to run in fear, some toward the exit, some toward the back room, and some toward the king's throne, where the goblins were crawling on top of each other to get out of the way.

"So, hurt my sister, will you?" Lily boomed.

Lily reached down and grabbed Sarah, picking her up carefully from the hands of the goblins that had hoisted Sarah up to put her over the fire. With her other hand, Lily reached down and grabbed the fat little goblin king, who was still tongue-tied by what had happened.

"Grraaawwwwrrrr," she roared at the other goblins on the ground, sending them scurrying under tables and out doors. Lily pushed the remaining goblins out of the way and stepped toward the exit. When she got there, though, she knew that she would never get more than her elbow out the door. But perhaps Lily could put Sarah down, so she could get away. Lily leaned over and looked out the door, and a mass of goblins was in the tunnel. Sarah would never make it. Lily lifted the goblin king up near her mouth.

"All right, you! This way is blocked. Is there another way my sister can get out?'

"No, that is the only way."

Sarah and Lily both knew he was lying, so Lily gave him a little squeeze with her hand.

"STOP! No, there is another way. Behind my throne! Behind my throne, there is a door that leads to my personal escape tunnel."

Lily pushed through the crowd until she was near the throne. She then pushed all the little goblins out of the way so Sarah could get away.

"Lily, watch out behind you," Sarah said.

It was when Lily's back was turned that the goblins began to make their move. Several rows of goblins in armor and spears lined up at the exit. A goblin—it looked like Hoblob, the goblin who had argued with the king—was organizing the troops and driving them toward Lily.

"Kill the giant!" he yelled.

A line of spears flew through the air, and several found their mark, mostly in Lily's clothes. However, one stuck in her leg, and another hit her hand, forcing her to drop the king. He scrambled off to safety behind the ranks of the goblins. The little spears did not make Lily bleed, but they hurt like the dickens. It was like several little pin pricks, only the pin remained in Lily's skin. Lily stopped and pulled the spears out of her leg and hand. As she did, another row of goblins came forward with spears at their ready. Hoblob shouted out another order, and the goblins all pulled back their spears to throw. Lily put Sarah down and threw her arms up in front of her. She knew that she would not be able to take much more. Soon, she would not be able to retaliate because of the pain, and they would move in with their swords and cut her up, piece by giant piece.

Lily began to cry. She could not help it. They were such mean little things. They should have given up when they saw her so big or at least run away. Not stay and fight. Now, they were going to kill her. Lily had only provided them with more to eat, which made her even sadder. The tears began to roll down her cheek.

"Get away while you still can, Sarah," Lily said.

"I'm not going to leave you," Sarah said.

As Lily continued to cry and sob, the goblins suddenly stopped what they were doing. No spears flew through the air. There seemed to be some kind of disturbance or distraction in the goblin lines. Lily opened her eyes and looked over her shoulder. The goblins at the rear were shouting, and the lines were re-forming facing toward the door.

Arrows began flying through the door, and the goblins started to back up as several dropped with feathered shafts sticking in them. A shield line formed as a full battle was starting. A group of elves pushed through the door, their bows at the ready. Next to them flew little balls of light that Sarah and Lily knew were pixies and sprites. The fairies had come!

Soon, the arrows had pushed the goblins back far enough for the elves and fairies to form a line of their own. More were flooding into the room. Dwarves bearing axes and pickaxes formed a shield line behind which elven archers could stand without fear of the goblins. Next came foxes, lynxes, and wolves with gnomes or other fairies on their backs. One large fox had a mouse on its back. It was Elwin! The new arrivals lined up like cavalry and started to ride down on the flank of the goblin lines. The battle was on. They clashed several times, with many elves and goblins falling. But as more and more elves pushed into the room, the goblins were soon outnumbered.

Realizing their fate, the goblins tried to retreat toward the door near Sarah and Lily. Thinking fast, Lily picked up some tables and blocked the door. The goblins reacted by charging at her in desperation. Lily retreated into the far corner in front of Sarah, pulling up her arms and legs in a ball to protect them from attack. Before the goblins reached them, the elves and fairies cut the goblins off, forming a new line in front of Sarah and Lily.

The two lines of elves and fairies advanced on the goblins. Sensing their defeat, most of the goblins fled out the door. Since goblins don't believe in surrender, especially to elves, the handful that remained continued to fight until none were left. The two lines met. Within minutes, there were no goblin left in the room, not even the king, who had fled out into the hallway with the first group that escaped into the hall. Even the bodies of the fallen had been removed by the fairies and elves. The hall was picked clean.

Several fairies left the hall to hunt down the goblins that made it out the door. Across the room, a fox rode up to Lily, and Elwin jumped off its back. He ran up to the girls waving and shouting. Sarah picked up Elwin, and Lily picked up Sarah.

"I'm so glad you are all right," Elwin said. "We did not know whether you would still be alive, the way goblins treat their prisoners."

"It was the witch's orders that we be kept alive," Sarah said.

"And where is the witch? We expected her to be here, too, and to have to fight off her magic as well as the goblins."

"The fairy dragon got her," Lily said. Sarah quickly explained all that happened since they arrived.

"And you found our trail, OK? We tried to leave a lot of things for you to follow, so you would know which way we went," Sarah said.

"I left some things, too," Lily said.

"That was quick thinking. If it had not been for that, it might have taken us days to find you instead of a couple of hours," Elwin said.

"Yes, tell us how you found us," Sarah and Lily requested.

Elwin explained, "I jumped off of you before the goblins noticed me and ran into my mouse hole. After I watched where they took you, I went into the forest and shouted 'Mulberry' three times, as you told me to do. A guard found me and took me to the Fairy Queen. I told her what had happened, and she immediately assembled her army, calling on the elves, sprites, gnomes, and other fairy people that lived close at hand. The queen even got the dwarves involved. Although they traditionally do not get along with elves, they hate the goblins more than anyone because the goblins delve into their realm—the earth—and steal their gold. I led the fairy army into the barn where the hidden staircase was, and we started to follow. When we got to the first intersection, we did not know which way you had gone. But a scout saw the beads you left down one of the passages. From that point on, we simply looked for the clues you left at every turn, and pretty soon we were here.

"That's when it got interesting. Goblins, trolls, or their allies inhabited several of the rooms near this cavern. It seems the witch was gathering all the wicked peoples she could to make a try at conquering the Kingdom of Fairie. Luckily, because of the feast that was going on, most of them were in the cavern, so we were able to approach without running into too many creatures. We did a room-by-room search, taking care of one goblin at a time, until nothing was left to search but this cavern and the rooms coming off of it. We approached stealthily, and our scouts—two sprites that turned themselves invisible—saw what was happening to you, and we charged into the room. The rest you know."

Since parties of elves and fairies would be hunting goblins all night long, Elwin suggested that they find someplace to lie down and rest. With Lily being so big, she could not fit out the door, so the girls finally decided to just lie down in the cavern. Because of all the fairies running and flying about, they had no need to worry about protecting themselves if the goblins returned. And since both Sarah and Lily were so exhausted, they went right to sleep despite the ongoing commotion.

19

Restoration

The next morning, after Sarah and Lily ate a good fairy breakfast and drank and washed using the water the elves brought (the goblin water being so dirty), the fairies finally began to assemble.

"What is going on?" Sarah asked.

"The queen is coming," someone answered.

They joined the crowd, and a few moments later, the Fairy Queen, accompanied by her guards, flew into the room. All of the elves and sprites bowed low before her. Once inside, she gradually grew larger until she was the size of Sarah's mother.

"Princesses Sarah and Lily," she said, walking up to them.

"Princesses?" Elwin said, looking at them both with a renewed sense of wonder.

"Did you fulfill the mission?" Queen Selena asked.

"Yes," Sarah said.

"And the child?"

"Sarah has him in her pocket," Lily said. Sarah reached into her pocket and pulled out the tiny quartz pebble in the shape of a child. The queen held out her hand and took the quartz from Sarah. With only a brief glance and a smile of joy that every parent would know, she gave it to one of her courtiers, who put it into a chest and promptly locked it.

"Since we are still in danger, let us not speak of this any more until we are back in the safety of our own house," Selena commanded.

Selena then curtsied majestically before them, and took Sarah's and Lily's hands. "You have both done us a tremendous service that we will never be able to repay. You took on yourselves greater danger than even we had asked simply out of the duty you felt to your fellow beings. Bless you both."

The queen looked up at Lily. "I see you have used the gifts I gave you wisely. Lily, you must be the first one we restore, since you cannot leave until we do. Then, we should leave this nasty place and go where we can concentrate on what must be done to set things right."

Standing in front of Lily, who towered over her, Selena clapped her hands over her head and held them up in front of her with palms out. Lily began to shrink slowly until she was fairy size. Selena did the same with Sarah, who also shrank back to fairy size so that both girls could travel with the fairy entourage. Then, the queen clapped her hands twice and two elves entered carrying a small trunk. The queen opened it. Inside were clean clothes—dresses, shoes, jewelry, and more—all in Sarah's and Lily's sizes. Another elf stepped forward with a basin and towels, and two more brought in a folding screen.

"Please, change from your travel—and war-worn things. Then ride with me back to our palace. Elwin will accompany us."

The girls did as she asked, washing their faces and arms before putting on the clothes. They were glad for the change, for nothing feels as good as a nice wash and a fine suit of clothes after having worn the same dirty clothes for such a long time.

When the girls had changed, the queen took their hands in hers, and they walked toward the door. As they did, the queen lifted them off the ground as she took to wing. Without any effort, they were flying with Selena. A whole company of fairies flew next to them, some bearing shields and spears and some with bows, all flying in formation. Next to them, two sprites carried Elwin gently in their arms.

Leaving the goblin halls took less time than getting there, presumably because of their glad hearts, but also because they flew much faster than even the goblins had forced Sarah and Lily to march. Before sundown, they had arrived at the witch's cottage. The door was still standing wide open from their hasty departure less than two days before. They went inside briefly as Sarah, Lily, and Elwin recounted to the queen all that had happened there.

The queen posted guards all about the house.

"What are you going to do to her house, destroy it?" Lily asked.

"No, for she would return and try to rebuild in the ruins, or else her servants would turn it into some kind of shrine. The best way to keep her and her minions from coming back is to have someone trustworthy occupy the house. Of course, we will fill in the holes and tunnels so that any goblins that survive below cannot get out this way."

"Just as long as it's not me that has to stay here," said Elwin under his breath. "I lived here long enough."

After a brief sojourn, the party continued on their way over the ground at a more leisurely pace. It was an enormous train, complete with mice and rabbits carrying supplies, and dwarves, elves, gnomes, and pixies following in tow. They seemed to be taking a route that led them close to the road they took to the lake, although they avoided the Whispering Pines and other dangers. Along the way, Sarah, Lily, or Elwin would say, "Remember when we stopped here overnight," or, "That's where we ate lunch at such and such a time." Even though it was only a few days ago, it seemed like it had been a year. After each day, the fairies would stop and put up a tent—not a pup tent, but a large tent for royalty with furniture and rugs and lots of pillows. Then they would make a feast each night at a long dinner table that one of the rabbits carried.

Queen Selena spoke to them along the way about their adventures, asking for detailed descriptions of each encounter. She had a cartographer make a map showing where the dragon's domain was, where the brownie lived, and where the island was.

"While your part in the battle is over, the war will go on for some time. We must send troops to round up all of the witch's allies, such as the brownies. We will have to send someone to find out from the fairy dragon what happened to Fiara—I may take care of this myself. We will also have to make a thorough search of the island to make sure the witch has not held any other fairies there."

Selena continued, however, to remain silent about the fairy child or the wand. When Sarah tried to raise the subject, she would only say, "We are still in the witch's realm. Let us wait until we are far from here."

After about three days, the troupe made it to the river that fed the lake, and around dusk they crossed over on small boats disguised to look like animals or even logs. One was shaped as a swan, another as a duck, and some as fish with heads sticking out of water. That way, people who saw them thought that only animals or driftwood passed by.

It was a pleasant cruise. The boats were equipped with all the amenities, including food and drink, tables and chairs to sit and eat, and even musicians. They feasted all throughout the night, and when it got late, the servants showed Sarah and Lily to a chamber on one of the boats containing a bed, where they slept until morning. The girls woke with the dawn and saw the north shore of the river only a few hundred yards away.

When they arrived on the far side, their caravan continued. Now, the way was becoming more familiar. They passed buildings they recognized, and by the second day from the river, they were back at their own yard. They made straight for the stump where the fairies hid their palace. Finally, they had made it back home.

That evening, after they had all supped on the wonderful fairy food, the queen bid them sit on chairs next to her throne to talk. She motioned to her courtiers to bring forth the chest. They did so, and unlocked it, pulling out the now large white crystal. Selena picked it up and held it in her hand, tears running down her cheek. Sarah could only think of the restraint it took to wait.

"Now, let us see the wand," Selena said.

Sarah reached behind her back and produced the long, metallic rod. She handed it to the queen, who looked at it carefully, noting the markings on it.

"Call Haman," Selena said. One of the courtiers left to get him. "He is the court magician," the queen explained to them. "I do not know enough about the wand to dare use it, but Haman has been studying the matter since Elwin told us about the wand and what Fiara did to all those fairies. Haman is very knowledgeable about such things."

Soon, Haman arrived. He was a tall, skinny elf with a long face and large pointed ears poking from under his pointed hat.

"Haman," the queen said, "here is the wand. Please inspect it and let me know if you think you can use it to undo the witch's spell."

"Yes, your highness." He picked up the wand and held the end up to his eye. He read the markings on the side. He twirled it around in his hand, making sure not to point it at anyone. Finally, he turned to Selena and said, "Yes, this is the wand of Qua'lin, the conjurer from the East, from whom Fiara had stolen it. It is the wand of transformation, as Elwin correctly stated. Fortunately for us, the spells of transformation were solely due to the magic of the wand, not any ability inherent in Fiara. Therefore, if I can operate the wand—and I should be able to since I received instruction from Qua'lin while you were away—then we should face no difficulty in undoing her spell."

The girls looked at Haman, wondering exactly what he said. And they wondered what sort of creature this Qua'lin was.

"So, the answer is yes?" the queen asked, to clarify for the girls' sake.

"Yes."

"Please do so, then, starting with Elwin."

Haman took the wand, and, waving it, he said some phrase under his breath, and the mouse disappeared in a flash, leaving a short little elf. In many ways, the elf that now stood before them resembled his mouse self, with a rather pointed nose, a scrawny mustache like whiskers, big round ears, and gray eyes. Sarah often wondered about how one always seemed to keep certain features no matter how bad things obscure your true self. Elwin thanked Haman and the queen profusely, bowing low to the ground. What little clothing he wore as a mouse now hung loose on him, barely covering him. Were it not for the cloak he had made, it would have been indecent.

"Please go change into more comfortable clothing," Selena said, "then return. We have more to discuss. I have a mission for you."

Elwin bowed and then left to follow a servant to another room.

"Now, Haman," she said turning to the elf lord once again, "Please restore the fairy child."

Haman walked over to the crystal, waved the wand over it, and said some magic words. The crystal began to glow white, soon brightening the whole room. Gradually, the light dimmed, and a young fairy was lying on the floor. At first, they wondered whether being stone all that time had damaged him because he just lay there minute after minute. Then, the child began to move his wings and extend his legs. Then he sat up and stretched. He was only asleep. When he was fully awake, he looked around. His bright eyes moved from one person to the next until he saw Selena.

"Mother!" he said, getting up and running to her.

"Yavonne!" she cried, running to him and taking him in her arms. They held each other for several minutes. Sarah and Lily watched, tears welling in their eyes from seeing such a touching reunion.

By the time that Elwin had returned, Selena had dried her eyes and sat talking with Yavonne, who was sitting on her lap, telling him about all that had happened after the witch had turned him to stone.

"It's amazing," Selena said to the girls. "The spell has had no ill effect, either aging or any kind of lingering paralysis. In fact, he does not remember anything that happened at all. It was as if we were still in the forest before the goblins attacked. It will take several days for him to understand all that has occurred."

Elwin walked up wearing a silk shirt, green leggings, a leather jerkin and boots, and a long green cloak. He now had a real sword at his side. Sarah and Lily ran to him to hug him and hold his hand.

Selena looked up and saw Elwin standing next to the girls.

"Ah, Elwin. I am glad to see you have returned and are looking so well. You have said that Fiara—the witch—turned many fairies into stones or other animals?"

"Yes, your majesty."

"And you saw this with your own eyes?"

"Yes, your majesty."

"Seeing that you were an eye witness to this crime and know at least some of the fairies involved, I must ask for your continued help. Someone must go to the woods near the witch's cottage and return to the island to look for these transformed fairies that we may restore them to their original form. You will have to look throughout the yard for any stones or objects that don't belong, or other creatures that may be transformed fairies. Every stone on Crow's Island must be checked. Every fairy we can find must be restored."

"But I know no magic," said Elwin.

"That is why I will send Haman with you. He has control of the wand and knows a lot of magic beyond its use. He is very knowledgeable about magic and can perhaps help to identify magical objects in the witch's domain.

"And since I do not want the wand falling into evil hands again, I will also send soldiers to help guard you from evil. I have no doubt that it will be perilous since many would like to get their hands on the wand. There are many of the witch's servants out and about, hiding and perhaps awaiting her return. It will be dangerous, but it is only right that we try to undo as much of the evil that the witch did as we can. After that, we must destroy the wand to prevent its use in such a wicked plot again. That way, no one will be able to use the wand against my peoples again. Have we already made arrangements with Qua'lin to destroy the wand?" Selena asked.

"Yes," said Haman. "Qua'lin agrees and regrets that his wand caused so many troubles to so many people. We must destroy the wand with lightning, for that was how it was made. I already have a plan in place to do just that. I have a lightning rod, which Sarah described to me. We can place the rod far from any fairy dwelling to draw lightning to destroy the wand."

"Good. Now, is there anything else that you require to complete this mission?" Selena asked.

"Your majesty, I would only ask that you give me a few weeks' leave to set my affairs in order once more. After all,

I have been absent for almost a year. And I would like to return to my home, restore my lands so that I may have food in the coming winter, and reconnect with my friends and family," Elwin said.

Suddenly, Sarah and Lily realized that their adventure had come to an end. They looked sadly at Elwin and then at the queen.

"Of course," Selena said. Then turning to Sarah and Lily, she added, "I know your thoughts, and, no, you need not leave immediately. We can slow time for your mother for a little while longer. That will give you time to heal of any hurts, and for us to show you our appreciation. Which brings me to my next question. What would you have as a reward for your service to us?"

Sarah thought for a moment. "You have already made us princesses among your people and named us elf friends. Does that mean that we can return when we want?"

"Any time you want," Selena said.

"That is all that I could wish for . . . to visit my friends when I am lonely and miss them, to keep track of their lives, and continue to be of service to you and your son."

"A truly wise and unselfish request," Selena said. "For now you can have riches, food, or clothes—all the things you might possibly desire—any time you want, although you will not be able to take them back to your world. All you need to do to visit us is seek for us near the stump and say my name three times. When you return to us, you will always live as princesses, as indeed you truly are. And you will have our eternal gratitude, love, and affection."

Then turning to Lily, Selena said, "And you, Lily, what would you want?"

At first, Lily had thought about the clothes, food, and jewelry, but Sarah's wish had made wishing for those things unnecessary. She thought about everything she might want.

"I want to be back home again, with my Mommy and Daddy, in the house I love, and for us to be happy as we never have been before."

"Another wise wish," the queen said. "It shall be done as soon as you are ready to leave."

20

Home Again

Sarah, Lily, and Elwin stayed at the palace of the Fairy Queen for several more days. Each day, they would go out with the fairies—hunting, flying about the trees, riding the autumn leaves down from the branches, or just wandering in the late fall sunshine. Each night, they dressed in the finery the fairies had given them, feasted on the wonderful fairy food, danced the fairy dances, and listened to stories and songs. After only the second day, they had healed from all the evils they had endured—the terrible goblins, the dirty crows, the witch, and the long days of traveling and exposure to the harsh weather. Every sniffle was gone, every muscle was fully rested, and the terrible battle they witnessed was just a dream to be celebrated in song around the fairy fires. At last, Sarah and Lily knew that it was time for them to return home. At last they came before the Fairy Queen.

"Your majesty," Sarah said, "We want to go home now."

"I knew that you would come soon. You are now rested and healed. There is nothing to keep you from leaving. Tomorrow, there will be another market near your house. If you wish, you may wait until then to return. As you requested, you are free to come back to visit us anytime you wish. I would, however, warn you not to be too free in talking about what you have seen. If the big people find out we are here, there will be constant troubles. Adults will want to find us and capture us. Even telling other children could be dangerous because many wicked children would do nothing but torture our people, pulling off their wings or feeding them to cats. We have enough trouble trying to undo the magic of Fiara. We do not need a lot of humans nosing about, capturing our people, or destroying our homes."

"We promise not to say anything to anyone other than our parents, who we must obey," Sarah said. Lily nodded in agreement.

"An honorable pledge. Very well. Let's have one last feast before you go."

That night the fairies held the greatest feast in the long memory of the Kingdom of Fairie. Sarah and Lily were feted as the guests of honor. There was lots of eating, dancing, and toasting. Everyone thanked them, but especially Queen Selena, Elwin, and little Yavonne.

"My friends," Selena said in one of many speeches made that night, "You know how grateful we are for all that you have done. Let me add a few parting words. Always remember that life is full of battles, for there will always be evil around us that we must fight. Sometimes the battles will be difficult. You will undergo hardships and temptations. It will not always be easy to stand up for or do what is right. But with friendship, faithfulness, and love, good will always win against evil. Keep the course your hearts set, and do not waver. I have called you princesses because you always were princesses. In your heart, you are as noble as the highest king, for true royalty comes from within. Always remain thus. Do not try to grow up too quickly or spoil your hearts with evil deeds or thoughts. This is what true royalty is. A toast—to Princess Sarah and Princess Lily."

All of the fairies repeated the toast with their glasses in the air, and then they returned to the party. Sarah and Lily ate and drank the finest food and danced late into the night. Yet they slept until only just after dawn, when the old gnome, Gnicholas, woke them. The girls got up as with new life, and, casting aside the fairy finery, the dresses and jewelry, the silk sheets and fine china, they dressed once more in their play clothes and rode out to the fairy marketplace on the back of a rabbit. Sarah and Lily sat talking with the old gnome as the fairies set up their tents and started to buy and sell. As it had so many weeks before, the sky began to cloud up not long after the market opened.

"It is time," the old gnome said.

"Goodbye," Sarah said.

"Say not goodbye but until we meet again, for most certainly we will meet again one day."

Sarah and Lily hugged Gnicholas and then stood back as he passed his staff in front of the girls. Immediately, the fairies began to get smaller and smaller, until Sarah and Lily realized they were now their normal size, looking down on the fairy marketplace from behind a bush. The clouds suddenly became very dark, and they could hear distant thunder as the storm approached, just as it did the day Sarah departed. The fairies began to pack up their things and started to leave, some flying, some riding on mice or rabbits, and some walking through the bushes, crawling under dead leaves, or just disappearing into the grass.

The girls heard their back door open. They looked up to see their mother coming out the door. "Sarah, Lily," she called. "It's starting to rain. You need to come in."

They rushed to their mother and gave her a hug like they had not seen her in a week, which, of course, in fairy time they hadn't. She could only say, "My, you're affectionate this morning."

The girls went inside and sat down to a breakfast of all their favorite foods. They were very thankful. The fairy food was nice, but it was different than the food they loved. They had missed everything, from family breakfasts to their rooms to just being able to relax.

"So what have you been doing all morning?" Mother asked.

"Playing with the fairies," Lily said.

"Oh, that's right. Sarah was telling me about that game last night."

"But it wasn't a game. We were gone for weeks and had all kinds of adventures," Lily insisted.

"Now, Lily. We played together only yesterday. It's fine to play games, but do not take them too far," Mother said.

Sarah looked at Lily and shook her head. Lily remembered their promise and decided it was better to let things drop. At least, *she* knew she was telling the truth.

After the storm, they went out to find the fairy marketplace, with Lily thinking she could prove it to her mother, but there was not a trace. It was better that way. They wanted to protect the fairy folk from the evils the Fairy Queen had mentioned—greedy grownups and mean little children, not to mention dogs, cats, goblins, and other servants of the witch. So they agreed that if they ever found evidence of fairies, they would cover it up.

Sarah and Lily continued to be friends with the fairies for many years. Many times, particularly if they became bored or lonely, they would go and visit the fairies. Most weekends, they would go out to visit the fairies at their marketplace and buy some of their wares. On occasional afternoons, they would go just to have tea, so they were always back before Mother suspected anything. If there was a special occasion—a feast or visits from Elwin or Haman—they would get the Fairy Queen to suspend time for their mother so they could stay overnight. It was in this way that they learned how Selena had talked to the fairy dragon and learned of the witch's death, how Elwin and Haman had searched Crow Island and restored several other fairies, and how the elves continued to hunt down goblins, dark elves, and the cruel men who served the witch.

During these wonderful visits, Sarah and Lily were always treated as princesses with fine clothes, succulent food, and beautiful rooms. In the spring, they would attend the fairy dances, as they danced in circles on their lawn. In the summer, they would follow the willow-the-wisp of the lightning bugs to the fairy homes, where they would sup as guests of honor. In the fall, there was the hunt, where they would tramp about the woods and sometimes stay with elves in their hunting cabins. One year, the queen requested that they come because the Great White Stag had appeared once more in the woods on the edge of town, and they joined the hunt as it tracked down the magnificent beast through the forests near their home.

Of course, Sarah and Lily had many more adventures during these years. There were still many evils lurking about, especially in the witch's old domain. The dark elves revolted and battled with the other fairies for many months until the fairies drove the dark elves from their home in the darkest part of the forest. Goblins and trolls continued to come down from the hills and from under the ground to harass people. It took a long time to clear many paths for safe travel. Elwin, who became a knight in the queen's court, led many of these efforts, and sometimes he would ask for Sarah's and Lily's help. And there were always problems with the big people. Sarah and Lily often distracted them or led them away from the fairies when the adults got too close.

Just as Sarah got her wish, Lily also got hers. Once they got home and things settled down, their family was closer than ever. All they had been through brought out the best in them. After leading Lily and Elwin through thick and thin, Sarah became much more responsible. She realized that one person can make a difference, so she pushed her friends to help people more. And as Sarah became more responsible, her mother trusted her more to help with all kinds of important tasks. Lily, meanwhile, became much more courageous and honest. She saw that good would always overcome evil, so there was no need to fear anything but the wickedness of people, especially in herself. And all of their struggles had brought her and Sarah closer together, so that they would always remain the best of friends. Although friends who overheard their talk about fairies said they were only make-believe, everything the Fairy Queen said came true.

Some months later, Daddy finally came home from his military job across the ocean. They shared a lot of hugs and gifts, and eventually, life settled back down to its usual routine. But Daddy quickly saw that they had all changed, and changed for the better. They had grown up while he was gone. He even thought they were a little taller, although Sarah and Lily always wondered if in changing sizes so many times they ever got back to their original size. Perhaps, the girls thought, the fairies had left them a little bit bigger than they remembered.

But Daddy saw that they had grown in other ways as well. He saw how much more courageous and grown up his girls seemed. He could only attribute this to his absence and their having to learn self-reliance. He was truly proud of them.

That first night back, they all looked forward to story time before bed. Daddy started to pull a book from the shelf to read to them, but instead, Sarah and Lily said, "We want to tell you a story."

"OK," Daddy said. So they told him the stories of their adventures. They told him about Lily being kidnapped by fairies, about the Fairy Queen and the quest for the fairy child, and about the witch and the battle in her underground fortress. Daddy was very amused and asked a lot of questions about their stay with the fairies.

"What wonderful imaginations you have," Daddy said. Sarah and Lily smiled knowingly at each other. Daddy could think it was a game, just like Mommy. They knew it was real.

The next day, the girls went out with Daddy to show him where the fairy market was and the way to the Fairy Queen's palace. He played with them and talked about all he had ever read of fairies. As they played around the bushes, Daddy reached down and picked up a small stool.

"Sarah, you don't need to leave your doll house furniture outside," he started to say. "Wait a second. Look at the detail on this stool, etchings and gold gilding. I've never seen doll house furniture of this craftsmanship. This is really amazing."

Suddenly, Daddy looked down at their wide-eyed stares and smiles. Then he knew.

About the Author

J.D. Manders is a technical writer and historian who has written widely about technology and the history of technology. He has been a member of the U.S. Army National Guard since 1988 and has deployed to both Iraq and Afghanistan. While serving in Iraq in 2004, Mr. Manders wrote the *Fairy Child* as a way of connecting with his girls. He has been happily married for more than twenty years and has two wonderful daughters.